THE JADE STRATAGEM

MITCH HERRON 6

STEVE P. VINCENT

The Jade Stratagem © 2022 Steve P. Vincent

1

Something slapped Mitch Herron softly in the face. His eyes shot open, his body coiled and ready to strike... and he sighed. It was just his bunkmate. The other man had rolled over and flopped his fleshy arm over Herron's face, an unconscious gesture not worthy of retaliation, rather a hazard of life when living in ridiculously close proximity to dozens of other people.

Herron jabbed his neighbour in the side with his finger, which roused the other man enough to get him to withdraw his arm, then muttered, "Sorry, pal."

He closed his eyes, but sleep eluded him, as it had for most of the last three months he'd spent imprisoned inside the small hut. If given the choice now, in hindsight, bleeding out from a gut shot in the Philippines would have been his preferred option, better than this current hell on Earth.

Instead, after he'd been shot by operatives sent to hunt him, he'd been patched up at the Chinese Embassy and then flown to China for a show trial. The whole charade had taken about three hours, with only prosecution evidence and witnesses presented in a closed courtroom to a panel of biased judges. The entire process was devoid of fairness and designed to railroad him toward one end point.

Guilt and death.

Since then, he'd done hard labour in a prison in the far west of China, awaiting execution. He'd been there three months – that alone was a triumph of sorts, because he'd learned the average prisoner usually perished from the appalling conditions within a month, saving the authorities the cost of a bullet. His survival had become a curiosity for the guards, but that didn't mean Herron was unscathed.

As he lay on his back, desperately trying to return to his slumber, he felt a familiar lump in his chest. A second later, he rolled onto his side and unleashed a barrage of violent, wracking coughs that woke several people and culminated in him spitting a gob of meaty phlegm onto the dirt floor. None of his neighbours chided him; they all had the sickness – whatever it was – and the evenings were an orchestra of coughing.

Tonight, it was Herron's turn.

Giving up on the idea of sleep, he sat upright and shuffled along the bunk he shared, doing his best to exit the bed making no noise, a small game he liked to play to remind him of when he put his skill for stealth and concealed movement to good use. Tonight, he made it to the ground without making a sound, although he wasn't sure whether the cough that preceded his escape counted.

He looked around the hut, which was illuminated only by what spilled in from the overhead floodlights outside. Like always, he was the first awake; every other prisoner squeezed every minute of sleep out of the night so they could survive another sixteen hours of tough work ahead. Given it was winter, this was doubly important, because the only time any of them could feel even the slightest hint of warmth was huddled together.

Worse than the cold was the stench. The reek of so many people confined in a small space would be bad at the best of times, but when those same people were worked half to death and denied the most basic sanitation, the combination was deadly. At the start of every day, like some sort of ghoulish alarm clock, the miasma of evacuated bowels signified one or two more had succumbed to the cold or hunger or sickness.

Which was another reason Herron liked to rise early – to escape the suffocating smell of death.

He'd survived another night, but as soon as he went outside to the lavatory, he could see in the bright light that old Mr Chi had not. His corpse littered the ground a few steps outside the door, half covered in snow, his lips blue and eyes devoid of life. He'd clearly taken the risk to shit into a tin bucket rather than in the hut's corner; that attempt to maintain the smallest shred of dignity had cost him his life.

Herron's practiced eye told him Chi had been there for hours. Not that the guards or anyone else cared. They patrolled on overhead gantries high above the prison grounds, armed with shotguns and rifles, rarely descending except to collect someone for execution or crack some skulls for crimes, real or imagined.

"Poor bastard." Herron leaned down to close Chi's eyes. He didn't bother to check for a pulse because even if he had found the barest whisper of life, the guards wouldn't help him. "Rest easy, my friend."

Although he was trained to be as hard as granite, Herron regretted Chi's death. He'd miss the old man. Chi had been one of the few prisoners who could speak English, and one of the few to survive in this place as long as Herron, a testament to the old guy's toughness. He'd been an enormous help to Herron from the moment he'd arrived, but now he was dead.

And his fate, after so many months, seemed an ominous portent of Herron's near future.

When he was finished with the lavatory, Herron stopped halfway back to the hut and reached down to scoop up some soft snow, the only source of clean water in the entire prison. He lifted it to his face and used it as an impromptu shower, running a handful through his overgrown hair and his scraggly beard, feeling colder but fresher for the effort. Then he put a handful into his mouth and sucked on it.

By the time he got back to the hut, the other prisoners had roused. Herron watched as they sat up in bed, rubbed their faces, and looked around to see who hadn't survived the night. A few of the older members of their little gang had passed away in their beds, including one who'd lasted barely a week. Several people noticed Chi's absence, and they looked at Herron.

"Outside." He shrugged, unsure how many of them understood what he'd said, although they nodded like they had. "What does it matter, anyway?"

"A little, I hope." A female voice spoke from behind him. American, as out of place here as a hamburger or a

Cadillac. She waited for him to turn, then smiled. "I'm Molly."

Herron looked her up and down, wondering for a moment if he was hallucinating. She was a young Chinese American woman, about thirty, with black hair. He hadn't seen her before, and her clothes were too clean for her to be anything but a new arrival at the prison, which made him wonder how the hell she'd got here.

When Herron didn't respond, she kept talking, as if she'd read his thoughts. "I arrived late last night when everyone was already asleep."

That made sense. Herron remembered now that he'd woken in the middle of the night to the sound of the door opening and the rush of cold air it had admitted. He'd quickly gone back to sleep, writing it off as someone headed for the lavatory, but it must have been her arrival. The fact she'd survived the night without becoming a blubbering mess suggested she might last a while.

He'd seen plenty of new prisoners in far worse shape, which didn't bide well for their future.

Still, he could tell she was putting on a brave face. Her eyes were puffy, which told him she'd been crying at some point and probably suffered through a sleepless night, but her lips were also slightly pursed with determination to gut her way through the first day and find some supports.

She persisted with him. "Don't suppose you'd be willing to show me the ropes around here a little?"

Herron figured there was no downside. If nothing else, giving her a few pointers would fill in some time before they started work for the day. "I'm Mitch."

"I know who you are." She smiled. "Let's just say the Chinese Government didn't like how I covered your trial, and I was too slow to get out of the country when it was finished."

Herron could have laughed. He could have laughed all day, all night, then still be standing here a day from now with a big grin on his face. After all his efforts to stay hidden during his career, he'd been confronted by a reporter in the middle of a Chinese political prison in the ass end of nowhere. It didn't matter a damn, but it seemed to signify he'd reached the end of the line.

Instead, he kept his expression flat. "Well, Molly, I'm sorry you landed in here because of me. I'd be happy to show you around."

What he almost told her but didn't was that there wasn't much to show. She'd seen the beds already. Soon enough, she'd see the work areas and the lavatory – a tin bucket that was rarely emptied, shielded on three sides by curtains hanging from a crude frame – and the paved area out front of each hut where they got two meals of rice and vegetable broth every day.

That was their entire world.

He was about to speak when the door burst open and the hut was filled with guards, who shouted in Mandarin. Herron stared at them blankly, but the panicked scramble around him told him all he needed to know. It was time for the weekly contraband check, a search that usually achieved little except to allow some soldiers to throw their weight around.

Herron didn't care. He had no contraband, so he simply stood in the line of prisoners and watched as the soldiers went to work. One, armed with a shotgun, kept watch while three more focused on the search. They tossed the threadbare blankets aside, flipped the thin mattresses, and searched each prisoner. Usually, they found no contraband and were content with making a colossal mess.

But today, someone had held onto a cigarette for a little too long.

It was always a gamble. The cigarettes were used in equal parts as currency and a desperate hit of normalcy, even for those who rarely smoked. In return for a little extra food or some other boon, the smokes found their way into your pocket. But the danger of being caught with them turned possession into a deadly game the inmates played with the guards.

Today, someone had lost the game of Russian roulette.

Herron kept his face neutral as the guard who'd found the single smoke held it up and shouted in Mandarin, his reaction over the top compared to the severity of the crime. But Herron's eyes did narrow when the shouts didn't stop. A murmur of panic rippled through the assembled prisoners that Herron didn't need to speak Mandarin to understand.

"Which of you is Molly?" The guard who'd found the smokes surprised Herron with his broken English. "Show yourself or else your cellmates will suffer."

Molly turned her head to look at Herron, panic in her eyes, then faced the guard and took a step forward. "Me."

The guard took his time to look Molly up and down. She was a rarity in the prison. A novelty. A young woman who'd not yet had her spirit crushed. He dripped sleaze as he sauntered over to her and stopped only inches from her. After a quick turn to his buddies to share a joke in Mandarin, he swung back to Molly, hand raised to strike.

Herron exploded with violence. He wasn't sure why he decided to make his stand now. Maybe it was because he'd seen this guard brutalise several others in the months he'd been here. Or because he was ready to hurry up and die. Or because his only friend in here – Chi – had paid with his life for the simple dignity of taking a shit in private. Whatever the reason, he was committed.

He took one step forward and caught the guard's hand as it was halfway to Molly's face. His muscles strained, but he stopped the blow entirely. The guard turned his head, shock and then outrage on his face, and Herron delivered a brutal headbutt with the crown of his head.

The impact hit the guard like a nuclear weapon hits a city.

His nose exploded, spewing blood.

His eyes went glassy.

He dropped.

Herron smiled at Molly for a split second, then focused on the other guards.

As the guards shouted at him in Mandarin, the other prisoners did the same, their tone a mix of excitement and worry. But any appetite Herron had for the fight disappeared instantly, when the guard armed with the shotgun turned to aim it – not at him, but at the tightly bunched group of prisoners.

Herron froze, and the guard smiled; he knew he'd won.

In a previous life, Herron would have exploited the guard's mistake and kept up the attack. By pointing a gun at the crowd, rather than him, the man had made a bet on Herron's morality and conscience. It would take absolutely no effort for Herron to charge into him and take him down in seconds, even if it meant a dozen prisoners ate a load of buckshot.

But in this life, he let out a lengthy sigh and spat at the guard. "You coward."

* * *

HERRON DIDN'T RESIST as one guard gripped each of his arms and marched him through the grounds of the prison, even as the morning skies darkened and the heavens opened. Heavy rain pelted down on him, making the chilly wind that roared through the prison feel like it was in his bones. His hair and clothes were soaked, and sticky mud from the winter's torrential downpours clung to the cheap, rubber-soled shoes he'd been issued.

As the rain increased, Herron was dragged deeper into the gargantuan prison, to places he hadn't been before in his three months inside. That a prison of such scale could exist seemingly on the periphery of the Chinese nation showed industrial-level suppression of dissidents and political prisoners, and that the regime wanted their detainees as far away from the power centre as possible.

Eventually, he was brought to a stop in a large open area, all concrete. All around him, the wooden huts used to house the prisoners faced in on the courtyard, which meant he was on display for thousands of other inmates – a mix of men and women. On overhead gantries, guards kept a watchful eye on the imprisoned masses, while at ground level Herron had his own detail of guards, including the guy whose nose he'd broken.

For minutes, then hours, he was forced to wait in the rain – a petty display to show him who was boss. The guards didn't care; they were sheltered under nearby cover, spared from the downpour. As he waited, Herron shivered, his body temperature dropping. His teeth chattered, but the whole time, he kept his head up and his eyes open. He refused to turn to the guards or show any weakness.

More hours passed, the rain heavy and relentless, until eventually it stopped. The black clouds were replaced with overcast skies, nasty and grey, although it looked like the prison would be spared any further rain for the time being. Five minutes after the last drop fell, a door opened on to the courtyard and a man emerged in full military uniform, sporting the rank of colonel on his epaulettes.

The Colonel strode proudly over to Herron, then leaned in close to his face. "Mr Herron, I know you're a big deal. But here, you are simply inmate 403605."

Herron kept quiet.

"As inmate 403605, you are at the mercy of me and my guards." The Colonel smiled. "And you made a huge mistake this morning."

Herron matched the smile, held the Colonel's gaze for a second, and then, just as he had with the man's subordinate, he obliterated the officer's nose with the crown of his skull. It was a brutal blow, delivered with all the pent-up frustration Herron had felt in his months in the prison. The Colonel grunted and dropped to the ground, knocked out instantly even as his nose erupted blood onto the concrete.

Even as the other inmates roared with approval and the guards closed in on him, Herron simply stood over the Colonel and laughed. Even as the expected blows from the stocks of the guards' shotguns rained down on him, he still laughed. Even as he dropped to the ground and curled into a ball, to prevent the blows from the guards from doing too much damage, he still laughed.

After a while, the guards stopped and hauled him to his feet, but the Colonel was nowhere to be seen. There was a trail of blood, so Herron assumed he'd been carried off to the infirmary, which was good enough for now. Glad he'd made a good first impression yet battered from the assault, Herron put up no further resistance as the guards gripped his arms and dragged him away.

He was taken past a dozen wooden huts, each with hundreds of men and women inside, until he was brought to a stop at a vacant field in a corner of the prison. He pulled up short when he saw who was already standing there in the dirt – Molly, a single armed guard monitoring her.

She was holding a shovel.

As Herron approached, still under close guard, she held the shovel out to him. "They told me to tell you, you need to dig. And that, if you stop, they'll shoot both of us."

Herron shrugged and started to dig.

Hours later, after all the daylight had been spent and the handle of the shovel he'd wielded for twelve hours was soaked in blood, he reached up to wipe the sweat from his brow. It was a futile exercise, given his clothes and his hair were soaked with perspiration, but he felt better for the effort, anyway. It was a slight gesture of resistance against the Chinese guards, who stared down at him from the edge of the pit he'd dug.

"Thirsty work." Herron looked up at one of the guards and cracked a wry smile. "But someone has to do it I guess."

His smile grew when the guard grunted a response in Mandarin. Herron didn't need to speak the language to understand the guard had ordered him to get back to work. He did so, mostly because he didn't want the guard to threaten Molly if he refused. She was sitting, cold on the ground in the middle of the pit, forced to watch as he put all his energy into the dig.

Herron assumed the hole he'd spent all day digging was for the concrete slab of a new prison hut. It was hot and hard work, despite the cold climate, and he hadn't been given any food, water, or rest. Even for a man with immense physical reserves, it was difficult to stay on his feet. Carrying the injuries from his beating, it was almost impossible.

But he wasn't done yet.

"Keep your spirits up." Herron dug the shovel deep into the earth as he spoke to Molly. "I'll still be on my feet when they get bored and throw us back into the hut."

"You sure?" Her voice was soft and uncertain. "If you apologise for assaulting them, they might reconsider and—"

"Forget that." Herron stopped his dig and turned to face her. "Think about the biggest asshole bully you've ever worked for and what would happen if you asked for him to go easy on you…"

She laughed.

Herron squinted. "What?"

"Ken Dinnane. He was my Bureau Chief in Beijing and if he was here, he'd be in charge of the place."

"If he's such a hardass, he should have told you not to cover my story." Herron frowned. "He should have known that too many questions would land you in here."

"Oh, he knew..." Her voice trailed off and a hint of sadness entered it. "He's the one who told me to keep at it..."

"Well, fuck him." Herron shrugged. "And don't let these bastards get you down, even when I'm not here to punch their lights out."

He drove the shovel into the dirt again. It was brutal to make her watch him be worked to death. He was a soldier and a killer who'd known the price of rebellion, but she was a journalist. It was a message to the rest of the prisoners and, once Herron dropped, the guards would make it her penance to her spread the word that dissent is death.

More hours passed, the sun replaced with portable floodlights, yet still Herron kept digging. A few times, the guards walked small groups of prisoners past the hole – no doubt the loudmouths and the gossips who'd help to get the word out. Because, while it was common for prisoners to die here, they mostly froze in their beds and simply didn't wake up. They were rarely so obviously worked to death.

Herron ignored the rubberneckers until a visitor he couldn't ignore arrived: the Colonel whose nose he'd broken. The officer sauntered up to the pit and shared harsh words in Mandarin with the guards. He was unhappy, either with the fact that Herron was still alive or that the pit wasn't fully dug yet, and once he had left again, the guards remained tense and on edge.

Herron gave a grim laugh. "Sorry to inconvenience you bastards. I'll still be here tomorrow. Will you?"

He dug more and only stopped again when the Colonel returned, deep into the night, to check in on his progress. Clearly, the man was heavily invested in his new building, or Herron's punishment, or both. But this time – to Herron's surprise – the officer walked right past the guards and to the edge of the pit.

"Enough of this." He spoke in broken English as the guards shone a flashlight down on Herron. "Put down the shovel and come with me."

Herron frowned. He'd resigned himself to the fact that he was going to die from exhaustion rather than in a blaze of gunfire, yet now the situation had changed again. He locked eyes with the Colonel for a second or two, deciding whether to obey or resist, until the guards again pointed their weapons at Molly and made the choice easy for him.

He followed the Colonel on a snaking route through the camp, Molly and the guards in their wake. They passed other prisoners; some looked thin and malnourished, others looked strong, but Herron could see an emptiness in their eyes that told him how brittle they were. A few unfortunate souls were broken in both body and spirit. They'd fall next.

On and on they walked, through fences and guard checkpoints, and the journey gave Herron a newfound appreciation of just how large the prison was. There were so many enemies China wanted as far out of the way as possible, or to punish brutally. It was a concentration camp, where those who entered were worked to death with no chance of freedom ever again.

It was the place Herron would die.

And he wasn't the only one.

His eyes narrowed. "You bastards."

Up ahead, dozens of prisoners had been lined up against one of the long walls that formed the exterior perimeter of the prison. Their backs were pressed hard up against it and their frightened faces were visible in the light that shone down from the guard walkway up above. Behind them, in the wall itself, Herron could see hundreds of places where bullets had chipped the concrete.

This was the place.

The colonel smiled at him, even as a dozen guards took aim at him. "Up against the wall."

* * *

HERRON KEPT his eyes open as he calmly waited for the end.

Around him, others were taking a different tack, though not necessarily by choice. On his left, a condemned young Chinese woman hyperventilated, so rife with panic that she could barely suck in any air at all. On his right, an older man whispered incoherently to himself. Yet neither dared move away from the wall because that would only hasten their end.

Even in their last moments, humans were hard-wired to behave in ways that would keep them alive.

If only for a few seconds.

Opposite them, twenty guards were lined in a long row, each with an assault rifle. The weapons were aimed at the ground, for now, but neither Herron nor the other poor schmucks beside him had any doubt about what would come next. They'd be shot and carted away, forgotten, until some other prisoners were forced to scrub their blood off the prison wall in a day or two.

The Colonel himself stood between the groups, then he walked over to Herron.

"Quite a statement you're making." Herron scoffed when the Colonel was in earshot. "If this is about me striking you, put a bullet in me or keep me digging the hole for the hut, but leave these people alone."

The Colonel squinted in apparent confusion, his mind clearly working overtime to translate Herron's words. Then he laughed. "You thought the hole was for another prison building?"

Herron frowned. "What's it for then?"

The Colonel smiled and held his hands wide to showcase the collection of prisoners like a game show host revealed a grand prize. Herron almost reached forward to snap his neck, but the guards raised their weapons and aimed them at people against the wall. Although Herron thought he could finish the Colonel before he was taken down, he didn't want to give the guards a reason to shoot early, end these people's lives sooner.

His hesitation simply made the Colonel grin wider still. "You're not the sort of man used to being restrained, are you?"

Herron didn't respond. His hands balled into fists by his side.

"Indeed, this is quite an inauspicious end for a man of your expertise." The Colonel got in Herron's bruised face. "The most wanted man in the world, shot dead in the backwaters of rural China."

"Shot dead is shot dead. Whether it's you or some other bootlicker pulling the trigger, it makes no difference to me."

The Colonel sneered. "I don't believe you."

Herron kept quiet. He was surprised it had taken this long to reach the end of the road. In his business, death usually came young and sudden. He'd put dozens of people in the ground. Hundreds. The simple law of averages said that his ticket would be punched eventually. When he'd struck out from the Enclave, he'd expected his life to be measured in days.

Instead, he'd rid the world of that plague, then enjoyed a few years in relative peace, despite being in the sights of every intelligence agency and contract killer on Earth. He hadn't expected to sail the ocean indefinitely, and although imprisonment and execution in rural China wasn't the way he'd have ended his own story, it was as good a death as any.

He smiled at the Colonel, enjoying his look of irritation. "Get it over with, you bastard."

The Colonel's face twisted into a sour grimace, clearly upset Herron hadn't buckled in the face of certain death. Then he walked away and left the guards to watch over the assembled prisoners, many of whom were now even more hysterical than before. Some cried, some pleaded, some stared at the guards, some stared at Herron, some simply stared at the dirt and waited for the end.

Seconds passed, then almost a minute, then longer. Any moment, Herron expected to hear the crack of the assault rifles, maybe a split-second before his own end came. Or he might be first. Either way, he didn't expect the guards to fire all on cue, because that required a level of precision and practice that was beyond a platoon of prison guards in the ass-end of China.

The longer he waited, the more irritated he got, prepared for the end but not for the cruelty of these people being forced to wait to feel the kiss of the bullet. A few of them pissed or shat themselves, an understandable human reaction. He himself didn't feel fear at the prospect of his death. He'd considered himself dead for a decade.

"Get on with it!" Herron shouted at the top of his voice. "Or in thirty more seconds, I'm going to charge right at you!"

The shots came, delivering death to the prisoners; men and women collapsed to the ground in their dozens, their lives ended.

But when the firing stopped, Herron was still standing.

He looked left and right, wondering why he'd been spared. Had the guard assigned to take him out been asleep at the wheel? Had his gun jammed? What other reason could there be for the fact that he was still alive when everyone else had fallen?

Then, instead of the delayed thunder of the assault rifle, he heard the distant bass rumble of a chopper.

The Colonel watched the helicopter close in, then he walked over to Herron. "I hope you appreciated my last gift to you before you leave my care."

Herron shouted curses at the Colonel, who simply walked away, leaving him against the wall, several rifles pointed at him and surrounded by corpses. The whole ghoulish show had been one final torment to amuse his captor.

The obvious question now: what came next?

Herron's senses tingled with anticipation as the helicopter landed, kicking up a plume of dust. A moment after it touched down, a side door slid open and revealed the same quartet of operatives who'd escorted him to the prison months ago. Two of them he knew from the Philippines – including the one who'd shot him – while the other pair had been reinforcements for the team members Herron had killed as they hunted him through the trees.

Then a fifth person exited the chopper.

Chinese Foreign Minister Han.

Herron knew his face. Almost anyone even remotely interested in global politics did. Han had been the spear tip of the aggressive Chinese push beyond its own borders and into conflict with others. Some of that had been direct, pushing into the territory or waters of smaller countries, while some had been more covert, like the undermining of the Fijian government by Chinese gas interests or sponsoring piracy in the Philippines.

Both efforts Herron had happily disrupted.

As Han exited the chopper, Herron wondered whether the politician had travelled to the prison to see the execution of a man who'd caused him so much trouble. Clearly, the Colonel had known Han was coming, and had never planned to have Herron shot; it remained to be seen if Herron was going to last mere minutes longer than his peers on the wall or if there was something more complex going on.

The Chinese Foreign Minister kept low as he walked

under the rotor and shielded his eyes from the dust and dirt being kicked up. But once he was clear of the chopper, Han surveyed his surrounds with disdain, a man used to the finer things, not the mud and the stench of a political prison at the end of the Earth.

Herron kept his eyes locked on Han as the politician scanned the crowd. Whether it was because it was dark – the camp lit only by the floodlights mounted on the walls – or because his eyesight was terrible, Han struggled to find what he was looking for. But when the Colonel approached the senior official and pointed at Herron, Han's face split with a wide smile.

Herron betrayed no emotion as Han approached, waiting until the man was close enough to hear before speaking. "You've come a long way to watch a condemned man die, Minister."

"Mr Herron, it's nice to finally meet you. But you mistake my intent. Things have changed a little since you've been in here."

2

Herron's eyes flickered open, but the sensation differed from waking up over the last few months. He had a pillow. And sheets. And a blanket. There was no neighbour to jostle for space and no corpses to worry about climbing over on the way out of his bunk. He was in a bed that was warm and a room that was quiet. For a moment, he was confused, a sensation he hadn't experienced many times in his life.

Then he remembered.

Since he'd left the prison in Han's chopper, he'd been flown to a local airport, then boarded a plane to Beijing, then transferred to a car and driven to a five-star hotel, then deposited in one of the rooms. The operatives escorting him had made it clear he was well guarded and that, besides the guards inside his room and outside his door, others were stationed in the rooms above, below, and on either side of his room.

Still, Herron's pride had demanded he try to escape. He'd checked the windows and the door – both locked – and then decided rest and recuperation would serve

him well until a better opportunity to escape came
along. He'd stocked up on room service, hit the mini
bar, taken a long shower, and then gone to bed.

Twelve glorious hours later, he felt like a new man.
At least until a wracking cough reminded him of the toll
the prison had taken on him, the grip of sickness he felt
in his chest and his muscles and his bones. He sighed.
"Time to figure out the cost of living."

He threw back the covers and climbed out of bed,
aware he had an imminent date with Han at the
Chinese Foreign Ministry building. He'd been told in
not-so-subtle terms that he'd better be ready by ten in
the morning or else the Chinese operatives would drag
him out of bed and toss him in the back of a car,
regardless of the state he was in. The agent standing in
the room – the same who had shot Herron in the
Philippines and had watched his every movement since
arriving at the hotel – was evidence they were ready and
willing to do just that.

He shuffled over to the window and pulled back the
curtains, bathing the room in sunlight. He squinted for
a moment until his eyes adjusted enough for him to
take in the view outside. The sun looked hazy, wreathed
by the smog and pollution of Beijing, the size and bustle
of the city beneath it a world away from the prison.

Like it or not, Herron was back in the big leagues.

He enjoyed the view for a minute, then made his way
to the bathroom, which was as big as the shower block
one hundred prisoners had access to together for five
minutes once per week. He turned on the heated
overhead light, ran the water, and stripped off his clothes.
When he'd showered the night before, he had been too

consumed by the sensation of the hot water and his own fatigue to pay attention to the toll prison had taken on his body. The kiss of the hot water on his skin had been close to the best thing Herron had ever experienced. After several months spent nearly frozen in a prison hut in rural China, the ability to warm up and wash the stink of his bunkmates out of his nostrils was an enormous treat.

Now, as he waited for the water to warm up, he turned to the mirror and took the time to examine what three months of captivity had done to him.

It wasn't pretty.

A face he didn't recognise stared back at him. His hair was shoulder length and thinner than he remembered, while further south his usually close shaved facial hair had sprouted into an unruly beard. In between, his skin looked pale and sallow, which contrasted with the heavy dark bags under his eyes, the deepening bruises from his punishment beating, and the deep lines on his forehead.

And that was the best news.

His body looked feeble. He was thinner than he'd ever been, thanks to the starvation and the sickness from the prison. Black and purple contusions had bloomed on his torso and arms, and it was a miracle nothing had been broken when the guards had gone to town on him. His hands were raw, scabbed from cuts and scraped skin earned during his time with the shovel. In fact, the only thing familiar about his body at all was the collection of scars earned over a few decades of combat: cuts and bullet holes that had long ago healed, plus one newer addition.

The bullet wound he'd taken in the gut in the

Philippines hadn't healed well. It looked as angry and inflamed as Herron felt.

With a sigh, he turned back to the shower and walked under the scalding water.

He spent more time in there than necessary, scrubbed every inch of himself, then did it twice more just to be sure. Even now, it felt as if layers of grime were being shed with each second he spent under the water. When he was done, he climbed out of the shower, grabbed the scissors and the razor he'd left on the bathroom counter, then got to work.

First, he used the scissors to cut most of the hair from his head and from his beard. It took a long time, but after a lot of work, he could use the razor to finish the job. He ran the blade over his head, removing every bit of hair, then he did the same with his beard. By the time he was done, his eyebrows were all that was left.

He surveyed his handiwork in the mirror and smiled. Where it was uninjured, his skin was a pale pink, scrubbed clean and hot from the water, while he'd also done a reasonable job of his hair and his beard. A few more minutes to brush his teeth with the hotel's complementary toothbrush was all it took to finish the job, and it finally felt like his rebirth was completed. He still wasn't quite himself, but the new model was an enormous improvement.

Only then did he turn to look at the operative assigned to watch over him. He smiled. "Enjoy the gun show?"

The Chinese agent stared at him, his face devoid of emotion. Either he didn't understand the joke, or he just didn't think Herron was funny. "Get dressed."

Herron nodded and left the room, a little

disappointed at the continued lack of banter with his guard. Although he was tempted to take down the man as payback for the gunshot wounds he had inflicted upon him months ago, he knew there was almost no chance of subsequent escape. The odds were bad, so he'd play along with their game for now.

Dressed in chinos and a shirt provided by his captors, he let himself be cuffed and then they left the hotel room. The same three operatives from the helicopter joined his room guard, and they escorted him into the elevator. Their pistols were clearly visible in their shoulder holsters.

The man who'd shot Herron appeared to be their leader. He was also the youngest of the lot. Herron had heard one of the others call him Wei, although he wasn't sure if that was a first name or last. Small and quiet, the man gave off the aura of someone who was the best of the best. He was the alpha in charge of the others.

When the elevator reached the ground level, Herron let the operatives lead him across the large open lobby and toward the entrance. Their little procession was gawked at by staff and other guests, which quickly resulted in the ire of the operatives. They snarled and barked at the rubberneckers to look away, while the few people who drifted closer were warned off.

The whole time the four men were focused on what was happening around them, Herron was focused on them and them alone. He knew the weak spot in any movement of a prisoner was between points A and B – less secure, less predictable, less contained – and he figured if he was going to make his move, it had to be now.

He was helped by the assumptions of his captors. To them, he was a broken man who'd already been thoroughly bested, who was handcuffed, and had no weapons and no resources with which to resist. And while most of that was true – except for the broken bit – Herron only needed an inch to have a chance at escape. It wouldn't be easy. These were skilled men, but he had one more advantage.

He didn't think under any circumstances they'd shoot him on the way to the meeting with their boss.

As they walked, for each step his captors took, Herron took a half-step less, subtly edging himself closer to the pair that took up the rear and allowing the advance pair a little too far ahead of him. The rear duo should have noticed, but with their attention diverted by the people all around them, they failed to spot it. The advance pair had no way to know because they were looking ahead.

Herron took a deep breath and steeled himself for the violence to come. When his left foot was planted on the ground, instead of another step, he rose onto the ball of his foot and then executed a perfect back kick with his right. The shot was high and on target, clipping the operative he'd aimed at on the chin and sending him to the ground.

Even before the man landed, and before those in front could turn to respond, Herron continued his momentum from the kick and swept the legs of the other operative tailing him. It wasn't a perfect shot – not even close – but his target had been focused on drawing his pistol and was unprepared to defend himself against the low blow.

The burst of activity had taken less than two

seconds, but Herron had gained all he needed to make his run for it. Both operatives behind him were down on the tiled floor, although quickly regaining their feet; those in front of him had turned and were drawing their weapons. He ignored them all, taking the opening his actions had provided and bolting across the hotel lobby.

Shouts and threats followed him, but the shot in the back he half expected never came. While he had no doubt the men would gun him down in public if their orders called for that, he'd correctly figured they wouldn't shoot him dead if their orders prevented it. He hadn't been visited at the prison by Han and then flown all the way to Beijing if the Chinese minister didn't intend to use him for some purpose or another. That meant Han would be pissed as hell if his goons got trigger-happy on the way to the appointment. Or if they didn't get Herron to the appointment at all.

As he ran, Herron heard the pounding of footsteps behind him, but he had escaped far worse circumstances with far less opportunity before.

HERRON KEPT his eyes down and pulled the stolen baseball cap lower over his head as he walked down Chaoyang Park Road toward the Beijing East Palace Apartment Towers. He was conscious of his vulnerability. Beijing was the epicentre of the largest authoritarian state in the world, saturated by an array of soldiers, secret police, and security cameras.

Not to mention the team of operatives Herron had left in his dust.

With his freedom won, the game had shifted to one

of cat and mouse. He knew every member of the regime, from Minister Han down to the lowest of lowly street cops, would now be hunting for him. He was now not only the most wanted fugitive in the world – a man who a few dozen governments had active kill orders against – but also a sore point of embarrassment for the PRC.

They'd paraded him in front of the media, put him on trial and promised he'd be executed, so it would be a source of international shame if he popped up on the streets of Beijing or elsewhere. He couldn't access an airport or a railway station without a hundred sets of eyes instantly being fixed on him. Hell, he could barely walk down the street without the threat of imminent discovery.

For a man used to living in the shadows, it was a new existence.

Arriving at the Apartment Towers, he removed his hat and walked up the stairs. The small, six-level office building had an entrance intercom, and while he knew it was a risk, he would need to show his face. He reached out, pressed the buzzer he wanted, then waited. All the while he felt exposed, like at any moment a cop car would pull up nearby and he'd have the authorities all over him.

Instead, after a moment, the intercom chime sounded, and a female American voice blared from the small speaker. "Yes?"

"Uh, Cara..." Herron's voice trailed off; he didn't really know what to say to this woman. "It's Mitch Herron..."

There was a long pause, so long Herron thought maybe she'd forgotten who he was or that she'd called the cops on him. After almost thirty seconds, she spoke again. "I thought you were dead."

"I get that a lot. Look, you don't have to help me, but I've got nowhere else to go and I need to get off the streets."

As he waited through another long pause, he looked away from the intercom to the surrounding street. Cars clogged the road and pedestrians in corporate attire bustled for space on the overcrowded sidewalk. Only a few people glanced at him – none for more than a second or two – and there were no cops or military personnel in sight.

Finally, a loud buzz sounded, and the heavy door unlocked with a clunk. Herron's attention returned to the intercom in time to hear the woman speak. "Come on up."

Herron took his finger off the intercom button and headed inside, taking the elevator up to the right level, then finding his way to the woman's door. He reached out to tap on it with his knuckles, but it opened before he could, revealing a tall woman with a hand on her hip.

"Why are you here, Mitch?" She raised an eyebrow, making it clear his entry hinged on his answer. "And don't bullshit me, okay?"

"I've never done that in my life, Cara. I'm on the run, I've got nowhere else to go and I need to get off the streets."

"You could have lied about that, you know." Her stern expression softened a bit. She sized him up for a second, then let out a lengthy sigh and held her arms out wide. "It's good to see you."

Herron wasn't one for physical displays of affection,

but he made an exception for Cara Sargent. Her husband, Declan, had been one of Herron's old special forces buddies. He'd also roughed her up badly, and she'd fled halfway across the globe to get away from him. As soon as Herron and his squad mates had found out about the abuses, they'd taken care of the problem.

She didn't know that, though.

Nor did she need to.

He pulled away from Cara and followed her inside, closing and locking the door behind them. She looked as well as ever and Herron was glad for it. It would have been easy for her to give up on life, given all that she'd been through, but instead – as best he could tell – she'd reset her life and made a success of it.

After he'd escaped the four operatives, he'd used a stolen phone and public Wi-Fi to track her down, a job that hadn't taken long given she didn't seem inclined to hide her identity or her business. She was now a powerful lawyer who represented Western firms in Beijing, helping them to navigate the maze of bureaucracy necessary for doing business in China.

And from the looks of her place, she was doing okay for herself: her open plan living and dining area was cavernous and decorated with expensive furniture. He froze on the spot and let out a loud whistle. "Good for you, Cara."

She shrugged and gestured him toward the dining table. "Do you want something to eat? Or something to drink?"

Herron nodded and took a seat while she went to work. He watched her work around the kitchen, deftly constructing a platter of food – meats, cheeses, crackers and fruit, a smorgasbord finer than Herron had eaten in years – and then complementing it with two glasses of wine. By the time she put it down in front of him, Herron's stomach had rumbled a few times.

He reached out to pick up the glass of wine. "You really know how to impress a guy."

She picked up her own glass and then took a sip. "What do you want, Mitch?"

"The wine and cheese were a reasonable start..." He let out a lengthy sigh. "Honestly, I need some cash and a place to lie low for a while..."

She ran a hand through her hair. "And then?"

Herron took his time to savour some of the food, although his eyes never once shifted from her. "And then I don't know."

As she continued to sip her wine, she sized him up, her face a clouded mystery of emotion. The only sound inside the apartment was the traffic noise from the street below, and her silence told him he was on his own. He'd come here out of desperation, because he knew nobody else in Beijing and had no cash. It looked like he might leave empty-handed.

Herron drained his wineglass and ate one more bite of food, then got to his feet. "Thanks for the hospitality, Cara. It was good to see you."

She didn't speak as he crossed the room, but when he was halfway down the hallway to the front door, she called out after him. "I'll help you if you tell me what happened to Declan."

Herron swallowed hard. He didn't want to tell her that, but he didn't have too much of a choice. Too many sets of eyes were after him to be on the street right now. He needed to hide for a day or two, let the heat die down and then make a break for somewhere a little cooler than Beijing. As a bonus, by then he might have figured out what he needed to do to get out of China.

If that meant he had to spill the beans on a job he swore he'd never talk about, then so be it.

He returned to the table, sat, and looked her in the eyes. "If you force me to tell you this, what comes out of my mouth can't go back in again."

"I know."

"Fine." He paused, just for a moment. "After Declan put you in hospital, he went on a mission with us. He didn't survive it. I can't tell you where or how, but he didn't suffer."

She nodded, stared at him for a long while. The silence was acute – almost painful – as this woman finally got the answer to a question that had no doubt dogged her for years. He waited for her to respond, the silence in the apartment matched by quiet outside of it... and it slowly dawned on Herron that there was a problem.

It started as a small warning in the deep recesses of his mind, but soon revealed itself like an emergency flare.

As Cara digested his words, Herron walked to the window and peered down at the street. The newfound quiet hadn't been his imagination and his mind had warned him accordingly. There were no cars on the street. No pedestrians on the sidewalk. He stared out for a good twenty seconds; it was like a major street of one of the most populous cities in the world had been frozen in time.

"What did you do?" Herron's eyes blazed with fury as he turned to Cara. "Who the hell did you call?"

Silence. Again.

He stalked over to her, smashed his wineglass on the edge of the table and held the sharp stem against her throat. "Talk."

"You won't hurt me, Mitch." Her features softened, and she stared at him with sadness in her eyes. "For what it's worth, I'm sorry, but they told me to call them if you came here and threatened my business if I didn't."

Before he had the chance to respond, the front door exploded on its hinges and the hallway was filled with Wei and the other operatives he'd shaken at the hotel. They advanced, pistols aimed right at him, sour looks on their faces. Herron sighed again, irritated that his efforts to escape had been wasted and that he'd been betrayed by the one person in Beijing he'd thought he could trust.

Even though she'd sold him out, she'd been dead right. He wouldn't harm her. Herron dropped the wine glass stem onto the ground and let himself be detained. This time, after his arms were pinned, the operatives cuffed him. They hadn't been bright enough to stop his initial escape, but they'd clearly learned their lesson.

"I hope business treats you well, Cara." Herron resisted the pull of the operatives, made a point of holding her gaze. "Because I don't think these gentlemen will."

She flashed a look of fear and her eyes pleaded for Herron to help her, but the damage had been done. He could no more save her than he could free himself a second time. She'd made a choice that had damned them both, but for now she'd be the one to pay the price for it. As he let himself be led to the door by the operatives, Herron noticed Wei stayed behind.

He didn't hear what the operative said to her.

* * *

HERRON TURNED to stare at Wei and smiled. "Your death is going to be my last flourish. It will be a masterpiece."

Wei's face was impassive, as blank as a white-painted wall, although after a few seconds the edges of his mouth creased into a smirk. "Good luck."

Herron glared at him for a second longer, then returned his focus to the office he was in. It was all timber and leather, the sort whose occupant got to choose exactly how it would be decorated, no expense spared. He was cuffed to a luxury wooden armchair, seated on the opposite side of an enormous desk. The operatives were spaced around the room with their pistols drawn and their attention unwavering.

There would be no tolerance for another escape attempt.

After he'd been dragged from Cara's place, he'd been bundled into a black van and immediately driven to the foreign ministry building. Upon arrival, he'd had more guns pointed at him than Berlin in 1945, and he'd made no fuss on the way to Han's office.

He was still struggling to digest Cara's betrayal and capture. It transformed the game. She'd been one of the few links left to his old life, the second he'd encountered this year, after he'd been rescued by Captain Jerome Laidlaw from his stricken yacht. This was different, though. Laidlaw was a soldier and the encounter with him had been pure chance. With Cara, he'd sought her out and asked for her help, but he'd been beaten to the punch by the Chinese authorities, who'd made her a better offer.

Now he was in a chair as he stewed and waited for

danger of another kind to arrive. And, thankfully, it didn't take long.

Minister Han entered the office and stood opposite Herron on the other side of the desk. The Chinese Foreign Minister regarded his prisoner for a few moments, then glanced at the operatives for long enough that they took a few steps back and relaxed a little.

"Nice to see you still look human after your time in prison." Han smirked. "That's important."

Herron scoffed. "I'm guessing you're not planning to put a bullet in me right away, then?"

"Oh, no, not right away." Han unbuttoned his suit jacket and sat. "Not before you complete a job for me."

"I'm retired."

"If you really think that, then you're a fool." Han rested his elbows on the desk and leaned forward. "Twenty years of foreign policy effort is about to culminate in the return to China of a grand prize – Hong Kong."

Herron's eyes narrowed a little. He knew little about the small island off the coast of China, but he knew one thing. "You signed a treaty with the British giving the place self-autonomy for fifty years..."

"Yes, yes." Han waved a hand, as if that detail was insignificant. "The local legislature has passed a law that requires the Hong Kong authorities to hand over anyone wanted by the mainland..."

Herron interjected. "A move you – and they – knew would trigger violent protests. Now you're ready to move in like the benevolent asshole you are."

He listened as Han rattled on, but inside he was fuming. All his efforts to foil Chinese meddling in Fiji and the Philippines had done nothing to stop their continued interference elsewhere. For a long while, the upstart superpower had been increasing its footprint in Asia using a mix of aid, diplomacy, and military pressure. Herron had seen it while he sailed the Pacific: smaller countries flipping their allegiance because they were induced or scared.

But this was different.

Since being relinquished by the British in 1997, Hong Kong had been a part of China in name only. A semi-autonomous region, it had enjoyed its own government and laws, its people substantially freer than their countrymen on the mainland. This status quo was meant to have been maintained until 2047, when the mainland would take over completely. The West had bet that the political situation on the mainland would be different by then.

China, however, aimed to shorten the timeline.

"So, what's the plan?" Herron crossed his arms across his chest, glad to be free of the cuffs, although he was no less a prisoner than he had been for the last three months. "Who needs to die?"

"If it were so simple, Mr Herron, I'd just have one of my people do it." Han sat back, steepled his fingers. "A few months ago, protests sparked by the new law gave me all the reason I needed to intervene. Thousands of Chinese police officers swarmed Hong Kong, but they have proven to be a spectacular failure in bringing the matter to a close. And so, we're proceeding with Operation: Jade Stratagem."

And that's where Han's briefing finished. Herron waited, but no more information was forthcoming.

"That's it?" Herron frowned. "You can't expect me to sign up for a job without knowing what it is."

For the first time since the Chinese Foreign Minister had bailed him out of prison, Herron thought he might be headed right back there. Han got to his feet, stared at Herron, and then left the room, leaving only one of the four operatives – Wei – to keep watch over the prisoner.

Herron looked at the operative. "Don't suppose I could get a coffee?"

Getting a blank look in return, he sighed and settled in to wait for whatever came next. Bored, he looked around. Just like in the General's residence in Fiji, he was struck by the contrast between the life of the elites in totalitarian dictatorships and the people they ruled over. At least the General had never made any claims to be a socialist. Nobody had doubted he was in charge and that he had power and privilege. Here it was different, with people like Han claiming they represented the common person yet living in opulence.

Herron wasn't sure, but he suspected no peasant in the countryside had a solid-gold ornate clock on the mantle of an open fireplace, which burned to keep the cold at bay. He doubted any worker worth his salt got to spend his day inside an office like this, larger than any apartment to be found in Beijing, with a staff of dozens to tend to every need.

But any further consideration of the comparison would have to wait. Han returned with a laptop under his arm, and Herron regarded him calmly as the politician placed the computer on the desk, opened the lid and punched in a password. After a moment and a few clicks on the track pad, Han looked up over the screen at Herron and smiled thinly. A career diplomat who knew he'd won.

And, to his credit, it was a damn good move.

"You bastard." Herron's voice was a whisper as he looked at the screen, which showed dozens of prisoners – including the journalist, Molly – in the hole he'd dug at the prison. "Let them out of there."

"Well, that's up to you." Han shrugged and then closed the lid of the laptop again, his message delivered. "If you agree to help me, they'll be let out of the hole rather than buried alive."

Herron seethed.

"And if you still don't agree to help me after that, your friend Cara will find her way into a hole of her own. But the choice is yours, of course."

"Of course." Herron didn't hesitate. Everything he'd seen of Han and his peers revealed the cruelty to do exactly what he'd threatened. He was stuck with no other choice. For now. "I agree."

The words felt heavy as they left his mouth, but Herron knew the commitment was only a theoretical one. Although Han hadn't told him anything about the job, the uncertainty ran both ways. He might complete the job if it was something he didn't morally oppose. But if it was something he objected to in that way – and he suspected it might be, based on the secrecy – then he was really screwed.

Refusal now gained him nothing and got the prisoners killed, whereas playing along bought him time to learn what Han wanted and foil it if given the chance. It wasn't a perfect plan, but it kept people alive and gave Herron options, which was good enough for now.

"There's an old saying from Sun Tzu: the supreme art of war is to subdue the enemy without fighting." Han shifted his gaze to one operative, nodded. "The prisoners will be out of their pit momentarily, and your friend will return home. But be warned, Mr Herron, any misbehaviour on your part will be treated... seriously."

3

Although Herron couldn't understand the protestors and their shouts for freedom, he was impressed by their volume. As he lifted a dumpling to his mouth and took a bite, he could hear them loudly shout their displeasure at their government's capitulation to China, even through the double-glazed windows of Din Tai Fung restaurant.

As he chewed, Herron glanced out the window. The streets below heaved like Times Square on New Year's Eve, the arteries of one of the central commercial precincts of Hong Kong clogged by the protests. It was like the entire city was frozen in the moment, with hundreds of thousands of demonstrators ringed by armed police, both sides ready for the spark that would light a giant conflagration.

Little did they know the guy supposed to light the fuse watched from up above them.

After he'd agreed to help Minister Han, Herron had been kept in the dark about exactly what was required from him. The only things he knew were that it would help China gain control of the island and that Cara Sargent, Molly, and a bunch of other prisoners would be killed if he refused. But as the moment of truth got closer, Herron was determined to find a way to sabotage Han's mission while also keeping those people alive.

But since leaving Han's office, Herron had been watched over constantly by Wei and the other operatives. He hadn't had a moment when at least two of them weren't observing him, and none of his attempts to pry information out of them had been successful. He had no phone, no computer, and no way to contact anyone or search for information. It was like he was on a rail – from the office to the target – with no way to divert.

He'd been flown to Hong Kong, driven from the airport, and deposited a few blocks from the protest. Now, in the heart of Hong Kong's main commercial areas – Causeway Bay – he'd been forced to quickly acclimatise. Given there was no hotel for him to stay at here, only an objective, it was a surprise he'd even been given the chance to eat.

But now his time was up.

As he took one last dumpling with his chopsticks, his babysitters stood as one and surrounded the table, signalling it was time to go. Herron looked at each of them, took his time savouring the last dumpling, then climbed to his feet. Just like at the hotel, two of them led off, while two of them followed.

Only this time, Herron knew that if he tried to make a run for it, Cara and the prisoners would be killed.

They walked through the restaurant, skirting the edges of a film shoot taking place around the kitchen area. A video camera crew was taking footage of one chef talking to a polished-looking presenter; some sort of food show, perhaps. And moving right behind them, Herron and his minders, off to cook up something far more newsworthy. He wondered if anyone would even care about their show this time tomorrow.

They headed down the escalator from the second level restaurant and out onto the street, which was filled with cops and protestors. As he followed the operatives to the destination, he took in the shouts of the protestors. Some were in Mandarin and aimed at Beijing, some were in Cantonese – the local Chinese dialect – and aimed at the chief executive in charge of the island. And some were in English and aimed at Western journalists.

"Our freedom is not yours to take!"

"One China! Two systems!"

"Hands off Hong Kong!"

The signs and placards in the street, some large and some small, were the same proportion of the two Chinese dialects and English. The combined effect was a sea of outrage, visible from one end of the street to the other, a veritable horde of concerned citizens that demanded the right to be heard and the right to remain free from the mainland.

But a quick glance around told Herron they'd already failed in one respect. He'd never seen so many police and high-tech security cameras capturing the faces of every single protestor arrayed against the mainland. He knew those faces would be catalogued by the authorities and those people would be dealt with later. A truly frightening proposition if the mainland won control of the island.

The further he walked, the more he sensed tensions

were on a knife's edge. One cop or protestor going too far could spark a blaze that would consume the entire island. It would give China just the excuse it needed to "bring order to the situation", to use Han's words, and deploy troops to crush the dissent once and for all.

It was a powder keg, and Herron had a sinking feeling he was going to light the fuse.

He followed the operatives down the length of the street, from Din Tai Fung to the very front end of the protests. The further they walked, the greater the space grew between them: the lead pair ranged ahead with no care for his position, while a glance over his shoulder told him the rear pair had lagged behind as well. Given how close they'd been to him in Beijing, it initially seemed strange to him, but the reason was clear.

They knew they had him in a noose.

Amongst the crowd and with such lax oversight from his minders, Herron spotted a hundred opportunities to slip away from them. It would be all too easy to lose himself in the crowd, go to ground in a back alley for a few weeks, then figure out whatever came next. But he knew – and they knew he knew – doing so would result in the deaths of dozens.

In his old life, Herron might have considered the price worth it, but not anymore.

So he tried to keep up with the operatives, hoping he might yet think of a way to avoid doing Han's job and still save the people at risk. But it was hard to do so without knowing what the job was. He'd made a deal with the devil ignorant of the terms of the bargain or the angles he might play to escape it.

He followed the operatives until they stopped at an unremarkable clothing store. It had boarded-up windows and was closed for business like many other small retailers in the area, yet when one operative unlocked the door and led the group inside, Herron knew it was key to whatever Han wanted him to do.

He was a little surprised when Wei handed him a flashlight and a backpack and gestured him through the open door. After glancing at the other man, then at the torch, Herron took it and stepped inside. Immediately, the noise from the street was dampened, an island of calm in a sea of chaos, and with the windows boarded, the store was bathed in inky blackness.

Herron turned on the flashlight, and the beam instantly cut through the darkness. Now, with the benefit of some light, he could see the store hadn't been open for some time, judging by the dust on the shelves. No one had even bothered to clear the stock, which was strewn about or hanging limply on railings.

The place had been abandoned quickly, then forgotten.

Now he just had to figure out why.

He used the beam to guide him past the racks of clothes to the back of the store, looking for anything that might give him a hint. He found nothing, so pushed through a saloon door to the rear staff area. As the door swung on its hinges behind him, Herron inhaled sharply. Suddenly, the reason the clothes store had been vacated was abundantly clear.

There was a giant hole in the middle of the floor.

Herron inched closer and was shocked to find it was deep. Very deep. The bottom was at least two storeys below street level, the depth of an underground parking lot or a large department store basement. It was nowhere near as wide, however, maybe enough for a handful of people to stand side-by-side at the bottom. And there was a bag at the bottom.

"Your job is in the bag." Leaving two of his men outside, Wei had entered the room with one of the other operatives. "Once it is completed, you're free to go."

Herron nodded, but didn't speak. He was stalling. From the moment he'd agreed to Han's little game, he'd been playing for time to think of a way out of the situation. Now time was up.

Ignoring Wei and the other operatives, he focused instead on the bottom of the pit. With the aid of his flashlight, he could see the tools that had been used – by God knew who – to dig the hole and uncover some copper pipes. He tracked the light around the outside of the pit until he spotted a rope tied to a wall bracket and hanging deep into the hole.

Herron climbed down it, his flashlight held between his teeth, careful with each inch he traversed down; he wasn't keen to fall and break his arm. Eventually he made it to the bottom and, after he'd brushed the dirt from his hands on his pants, took hold of the flashlight and looked around.

Ignoring the bag for a moment, he scanned every inch of the hole: the tools, the pipes, all of it. The first thing he found, up closer, was a square metal sign plate on one of the pipes. It was all written in Mandarin and Cantonese, with one exception: a company logo was stamped in the top left-hand corner. It told Herron all he needed to know because he'd come across it before.

China Offshore Oil and Gas Corporation.

A Chinese gas line was running right under the store, and someone had dug down to it.

Suddenly, Herron had a feeling he knew exactly what was in the bag.

He opened it and saw just what he expected.

A bomb.

It was large enough to ignite the gas line and blow up who knew how many city blocks before its fury was spent. Ten? Twenty? More?

Did it matter?

An explosion of that size was exactly what the doctor ordered for Han and his cronies. If the crime could be pinned on a Hong Kong independence figure, it would prove the need for a new local law allowing extradition of criminals to face Chinese justice. It was a trauma on a scale that permitted the mainland to act and prevented the rest of the world from doing much about it, especially if...

"Oh, you bastards." Herron shook his head in amazement as the last piece of a puzzle fell into place. "It's perfect."

He aimed the flashlight up at the ceiling and instantly spotted the bulbous black security camera pointed right down at the hole, no doubt recording everything that was happening in high definition. He was certain now there would be footage of him walking through the protests, then entering the store with the bag and the flashlight, then entering the store – all without his minders anywhere to be seen.

"Send in your troops to 'investigate' the incident," Herron whispered to himself, "then, once you're in control, release footage of a known western terrorist setting the device."

It would focus the attention of the world on the

United States rather than China's suppression of Hong Kong.

It was a plan as simple as it was genius, and it would give China everything it wanted.

They'd gain control over Hong Kong and delegitimize the protestors.

They'd avoid a messy Tiananmen Square-type situation.

They'd score a point against the United States.

Efficient. Clean. Final.

Unfortunately, Herron's unpacking of Han's plan came with another realisation: Cara Sargent and the prisoners were dead whether or not he planted the bomb. As potential witnesses to the set-up, they would have to be removed. The Chinese operatives already had what they needed – footage of him approaching the store and climbing into the hole. Whether he planted the bomb or not no longer mattered. If he refused, they could set it and blame him, anyway.

Cara, the prisoners, and Herron were all expendable.

* * *

HERRON GRUNTED as he pulled himself up over the edge of the pit and glared at the four Chinese operatives. Taking the flashlight from between his teeth, he said, "You bastards almost had me..."

"Almost?" Wei aimed his pistol at Herron. "We have exactly what we needed."

Ignoring the weapon pointed at him, Herron got to his feet. "I don't care, but I'd assume you'd want to be clear before the bomb goes off...."

Doubt crept in behind Wei's eyes, and the operative gave a slight nod of his head and a clipped phrase in Mandarin. One of his colleagues moved to the rope and climbed down, probably to check the timer on the bomb.

The odds arrayed against Herron were reduced by half now. Although Wei still had a weapon trained on him, he was alone at the rim of the pit, the two operatives keeping watch out front out of play for now.

Herron flicked off the flashlight.

The room suddenly shrouded in darkness, he bolted forward and shoved Wei hard in the chest. The Chinese stumbled back into some shelving, his shouts filled with surprise and frustration, but Herron had already left him in his dust, headed towards the front of the store.

The flaw in the Chinese plan had been having only one flashlight – any more cutting through the darkness and the security camera footage would show Herron wasn't acting alone. It had given Herron the only edge available to him. He couldn't stop them from setting the bomb, framing him, or killing their hostages.

What he could do was live to fight another day.

He expected Wei to shoot him in the back any moment, but although he heard his minder's silenced pistol pop off in the darkness, none of the shots found him. Locating the front door by memory, he burst through it, ran past the stunned operatives standing guard, and vanished into the crowd of protestors.

As the mass of people carried him away from the boarded-up store, the operatives would have no choice but to follow. They couldn't shoot him down in broad daylight, but they needed him dead, the only loose end in a plan that had otherwise been executed perfectly. Herron had to get clear, plan his payback.

He went with the flow of people all around him, a crush of bodies shouting and chanting and waving their placards. A few times, he looked over his shoulder for any sign the operatives had picked up the trail, but found none. With any luck, he'd be able to disappear completely – broke and stateless and framed for a crime he didn't commit, but free.

Which was more than he could say for the prisoners Han held hostage.

And Cara Sargent.

Herron barely had time to finish the thought when he sensed danger, an alert fired by years of surviving by his senses and intuition. Hyper-aware, and all his muscles tensed, he looked around, coiled to strike, but unable to locate the threat he knew was there...

He stood still in the middle of the crush, even as protestors stared at him and pushed past.

An arm wrapped around him from behind.

Without hesitation, Herron thrust his ass back into whoever had grabbed him, causing them to stumble back and release their grip just enough for him to break free. He turned and found himself face-to-face with the operatives he'd evaded out front of the store, both with their eyes locked on him.

Herron balled his fists by his side. "Didn't your mothers teach you that no means no?"

Neither said a word. Instead, they pulled back their suit jackets to show their pistols, an obvious message that if he didn't fall into line quickly, they'd force him to. He let out a long sigh, then nodded, letting them grab an arm each and lead him back toward the store. A few people around them noticed, but any interest in the situation vanished when they saw the scowls on the faces of his minders.

Until Herron made them take notice.

"Help!" His scream penetrated the noise of the protest and drew the attention of dozens of people. "I'm a journalist and these agents are trying to kidnap me!"

Instantly, the crowd's attention turned to him. A few seconds later, the handful who could speak English translated his words into Cantonese for those who couldn't. Shouts of protest were replaced with shouts of outrage about China's suppression of journalists.

Although he was usually allergic to public attention, Herron was glad for it now. He waited while a hundred cell phones pointed at them, limiting the options for the operatives. Han had already told Herron that China wanted to avoid a repeat of the Tiananmen Square massacre, which had led to international condemnation and required harsh suppression at home; he doubted his captors would cause a scene.

He was proven right. As the crowd descended on the two Chinese agents like a wave on a beach, they pushed and shoved back, but kept their pistols in their holsters. Their resistance was futile, the protestors more than happy to jostle back to help Herron, who they thought was a member of the Western press in need of support. In seconds, the grip on his arms loosened, and he moved away from the operatives.

Clear of them, he turned his attention to the bomb. Even knowing he'd indirectly given Han what he wanted, and likely failed to save Cara and the prisoners, he could minimise the impact of the bombing if he moved quickly enough.

He hurried over to a police officer at the edge of the crowd. "Excuse me, do you speak English?"

"Well enough." She shrugged. "What do you want?"

Herron let his shoulders slump with relief. "I heard some men talking about a bomb..."

He gave her the location of the shop, then slipped away as she spoke into her radio. Herron hoped she would set in motion an urgent search of the empty clothing store in time to foil the explosion. With nothing more he could do to prevent it, he melted back into the crowd.

He made it a hundred yards down the street, carried by the fury of the protest, the consequences of the last fifteen minutes heavy on his mind. Each step made him even more furious at the trap he'd walked into, and he focused on how he'd get back at Han and the operatives and the Chinese government.

Until the roar of an explosion interrupted his thoughts.

* * *

HERRON GRUNTED, knocked from his feet by a shock wave that sent hundreds of people around him to the ground, falling like dominos. The blast deafened him – even though it was several blocks away – and he coughed as he climbed back to his feet, his lungs filled with dust and grit from the explosion.

He ran a hand through his hair as he surveyed the damage. All around him, people ran from the blast; those who couldn't writhed on the ground. They were the lucky ones. As he looked back down the street, he could see hundreds who'd never move again, killed by the explosion or trampled by panicked protestors, or flayed by shrapnel and glass.

It looked like a war zone.

A hand squeezed Herron's ankle. He looked down and saw an old woman struggling to breathe. She was lucky to not have been trampled already. He would focus on revenge later. For the moment, he wanted to help keep this old woman alive and get her somewhere safer than here.

He reached down and scooped her up in his arms. She was like a fragile, wounded bird, thin and spindly, and it was a miracle she hadn't broken a bone in all the turmoil. There was little point trying to speak to her: language aside, she couldn't hear him, and he couldn't hear her. Instead, he focused on getting her away from the site of the explosion.

He walked slowly, careful not to trip over the debris that littered the ground. All around, hundreds of people flowed by him like a stream around a rock, but he kept his feet and received only a few incidental bumps. They made slow progress, one block at a time from the blast site, but he gradually got the old woman to safety.

He heard the sirens of emergency vehicles as they rushed to the scene of the explosion, the sound muffled, like he was underwater. At least it proved he hadn't outright lost his hearing, and soon, he could hear screams and shouts too – again muffled. He decided to try to speak a few words to the woman.

"Do you speak English?" He raised an eyebrow at her, then smiled when she shook her head. "Okay, you can hear me, but you can't understand me?"

The look on her face confirmed it: not blank, as if she could not hear, more like the confused smile sported by people the world over when they didn't understand whoever was talking to them. Unable to communicate verbally, Herron looked around and saw a real estate business on the ground floor of a nearby office tower.

He moved around some panicked protestors, until he was close enough to the real estate business for the woman to see him point to the picture of a house on the door, then to her. Her eyes lit up, and she pointed down the street. Best as he could tell, she'd caught wind of what he wanted to know – where she lived – and now he'd be able to rely on her to direct him there.

Herron couldn't help the great many victims of the bomb, and he knew the casualties would run high, given the bomb had gone off in the middle of a heavily populated area.

But one thing was clear: the gas line hadn't blown.

He did not know why, but that was the only reason Herron, the old woman and anyone else within thirty blocks was still alive; a failure in Han's plan that had saved thousands of lives. It wasn't a failure Herron would take for granted, however. The Chinese foreign minister no doubt had more planned for him and the island both, but it was enough for him to get out of the blast zone at least.

He carried the woman for blocks on end; she weighed very little, so it was no struggle. They eventually reached an apartment block where the woman used her hands to show that she was on the thirteenth floor. Realising there was no elevator, Herron groaned and started up the stairs.

As he climbed, the weird and wonderful smells of hundreds of people living near one another assaulted his senses. The delicious scent of food being cooked. The musty pong of damp laundry slowly drying in suffocating humidity. It was the same here as it was in the dense parts of New York or Tokyo or many great human metropolises.

Finally, they reached the thirteenth level, and the woman pointed to her apartment. It had a simple wooden door with a steel security grille covering it. Still holding the old woman in his arms, Herron kicked the grille, then waited. Soon someone unlocked and opened the wooden door: a man of about forty who immediately looked both relieved and shocked to see a westerner at the door with his –

"Grandmother!" The man spoke English, his tone thankful as he unlocked the security screen and opened it. "Thank you so much for bringing her back!"

"There was an explosion." Herron took a step back, and the man followed him out into the hallway. "Many of the protestors are killed or wounded."

"I heard. I've been worried sick." The man held his arms out and smiled when Herron transferred the frail woman to him. "She insisted on protesting for Hong Kong's freedom..."

Herron nodded. "Well, it almost got her killed. If she'd been a block or two closer to the blast, she would have died for her beliefs."

"And you don't think that's worth it?" The man paused, his own view clear. "We're in a fight for our survival on the island..."

"We?" Herron scoffed. "She was the one out there on the firing line while you were sitting on your ass."

The man seemed taken aback. He opened his mouth to speak, then closed it again, clearly unsure he wanted to take issue with the man who'd carried his grandmother to safety. The whole time, Herron simply stood there and waited for an explanation he usually wouldn't care about, as if it would salve his own doubts and insecurities about the bomb blast.

And his involvement in it.

"There are some of us working on the streets." The man spoke each word softly and carefully, as if to utter the wrong one could mean death. "And others who help the cause in other ways..."

"How do you help the cause? And how might I if I was so inclined?"

And he was very much inclined. The life he'd given up was a tough one, played for the highest stakes in the darkest shadows, but Han's actions had dragged him back into it.

Now, for the first time in months, he was a free man.

Free to hunt.

Free to hurt.

Free to kill.

He had no resources and no plan, and knew he'd be framed for the bombing. He knew it was a matter of time before he was captured or killed. It meant his only option was to strike with sheer, unbridled aggression.

It meant Mitch Herron was the most dangerous he'd ever been.

Finally, the other man spoke. "There's nothing you can do to help. This is our fight, not yours. Go home and stay out of it."

Herron frowned, but then nodded. It was a long shot that this man was any kind of organiser, someone who could point him in the right direction to help the protestors and their cause. It didn't matter. Herron would freelance. He'd just have to figure out where best to strike to damage the mainland's attempts to take control of Hong Kong.

He turned to go, but he didn't make it far before a voice called out after him.

"Mr Herron! Wait!"

4

Herron turned his head like a gun turret and stared down the mystery grandson. With menace in his voice, he said, "How do you know my name?"

The man took a few steps backwards into the apartment but didn't retreat completely. "Your face is all over the television…"

"Show me." Herron frowned. "Hey, what's your name, anyway?"

"Cheung."

Herron nodded and followed Cheung back into his apartment, where he saw a picture of his face dominating the television screen as a newsreader spoke in Cantonese. A second or two later, the picture shifted to security camera footage of Herron in the pit, which froze and zoomed in on his face. He was squarely in the frame for the explosion, whether or not he'd set the bomb.

It was something he'd expected, just not this quickly.

"You planted the bomb?" Cheung asked, his voice calm.

"It's a long story, but no." Herron rubbed a hand over his eyes. "Forget about that and tell me what they're saying about me."

"That you're a wanted man... you escaped prison... there's evidence of you planting the bomb... you're working for the protestors..."

There was another surprise. He'd expected the Chinese to blame the protestors, send in troops to subdue the movement, then show Herron planting the bomb and blame the United States. With the protest movement already crushed, it would allow China to re-direct the inevitable outrage of the international community toward Uncle Sam. It's what Herron would have done in Han's shoes, but the politician had cut corners.

"That'll do." Herron grumbled. "I know you probably won't believe me, but I didn't plant the bomb. Although they ordered me to."

"You think I believe the mainland's propaganda machine?" Cheung snorted. "If their state-run television said you did it, I'm certain you didn't."

"They broadcast that here?"

"They do lately." Cheung shrugged. "Anyway, now they're talking about some prisoners who are about to be executed in China for—"

"For what?" Herron's eyes narrowed and darted between Cheung and the screen, which still only showed the female newsreader.

"For aiding your escape." Cheung paused as the vision on the screen shifted to a familiar wall with a bunch of familiar prisoners lined up against it. "Or so they say..."

Herron's eyes stayed on the screen as the state news broadcast continued. The imminent death of the prisoners was spiteful and unnecessary, given Han's plan had succeeded.

It further reinforced his intent to strike back.

The image on the screen flashed back to Herron's face. "Keep translating for me."

"Uh, they're saying dozens of mainland Chinese citizens were caught in the blast... that you set the bomb to aid the protestors... that—"

Herron held up his hand to cut Cheung short. "I'm public enemy number one. I've sided with the protestors, they're all terrorists, and the authorities need to move in."

Cheung nodded.

Herron's lip curled in anger. He'd had enough of Han and the regime that had systematically taken everything from him, first in Fiji, then the Philippines, and now here.

"Hypothetically, if a highly skilled operative wanted to join your cause and help push the mainland's troops off the island, who would he talk to?"

Cheung hesitated... then the old woman said something in Cantonese. "She says that I need to trust you."

"Smart woman."

"Fine. There's going to be thousands of troops moving onto the island from tomorrow, so what choice do we have except to fight back?"

"Smart man."

"There's a briefing each evening where we discuss

the protest plan for the following day." Cheung paused. "We can't use any electronic means to coordinate with the leadership or they find us."

"Smart group." Herron was glad the protest leaders hadn't made themselves easy targets for China's electronic gophers to find. "Where?"

"I won't tell you that. But I'll take you there tonight. If the others agree to accept your help, I'll let you inside."

"Good enough. In the meantime, take your grandmother to a doctor and get her checked out."

"Okay. What are you going to do?"

"Oh, you know, the usual." Herron smiled. "Get some rest, have a meal and a drink, catch up on the news..."

Cheung helped his grandmother to her feet and headed for the door. "You're welcome to anything you need in the apartment. Take a shower and have a nap if you like. I'll be back soon."

As they passed him, the old woman smiled at Herron for the briefest second, even that simple gesture exhausting her. Herron smiled back before Cheung half-carried her out of the apartment and locked the door behind him, trapping Herron inside.

Herron was a little impressed. Cheung was clearly smart enough to keep the wild card in the box until it needed to be played, aware Herron might not stay put if given the choice. This way, Cheung would have time to get his grandmother checked out, but also to think about Herron's offer and talk to his peers.

Which is exactly what Herron wanted.

Waiting to be sure Cheung wasn't coming back, he sat on the sofa and flicked through the channels on the television until he found CNN. He watched the broadcast for a few minutes, finally able to understand now the reporters talked in English, but it offered no more solace than the coverage Cheung had translated. It was wall-to-wall reporting on the protests and the bombings.

And Herron was firmly in the frame.

With a sigh, he turned off the television and searched through Cheung's apartment. He was reliant on the fact that Hong Kong was one of the most hyper-connected societies on Earth, the lack of space for residents compensated for by a vibrant life online and outside the home.

He found a laptop on the kitchen bench – password protected – but then he struck gold on Cheung's bedside table, spotting an ebook reader.

Herron turned it on and, struggling to understand the text on the screen, it took him a few minutes to fumble his way to the settings screen. He changed the language to English and, just like that, he had a world of information and tools at his fingertips. For now, though, he was only interested in one thing.

He opened the email browser and typed out a message.

* * *

THE STREETS of Hong Kong were thick with tension as Herron and Cheung made their way from his apartment to the meet. The explosion and the imminent arrival of foreign troops had everyone on edge: eyes were downcast, voices were hushed, and every local on the street seemed in more of a hurry to complete their business and get where they were going.

Otherwise, Herron still found Hong Kong to be a wonder of human civilisation. The first time he'd visited a decade ago, he'd been amazed by the tiered layout of the city. Built to be harmonious with the natural sloped terrain, it meant the top of enormous skyscrapers would be at eye-level to people on a sidewalk just a hundred yards away, each level of the city climbing higher than the last.

Key to the city's successful operation was the enormous network of public escalators, public transportation Herron had not seen used anywhere else in the world. You could step onto the escalator at the bottom and, minutes later, have soared up to enormous altitude without a single step. Without the escalators, Herron wasn't sure how the city would operate.

Only twenty minutes after they'd left Cheung's place, they arrived. Their destination was a bar in a trendy part of Lan Kwai Fong that was dominated by western expatriates and tourists. Because of the humidity, the windows were all wide open and its clientele had spilled onto the street to get some relief from the heat. Within seconds, however, Herron could sense the scene was not quite right.

He turned to Cheung and fixed him with a quizzical look. "Nobody here looks like they'd be overly concerned about the freedom of your average local."

Cheung gestured to the bar's clientele like a game show host would showcase the grand prize. "Everyone is white, you mean?"

Herron's eyes narrowed, ashamed he hadn't figured

out the reason himself. "Impressive operational security."

By holding their meetups at a bar frequented by western expats and tourists, the leaders of the protests could be sure the only people of Chinese descent who got close were loyal to them. Unless the PRC turned one of the leaders, or got a tourist to work for them, they would be locked out of the bar. It was a protective layer that may as well be solid steel, almost impregnable.

"Wait here," Cheung said. "Get yourself a drink while I head out back. If the leadership decides you're welcome, the bartender will bring a beer."

"And if not?"

"He'll bring the cheque." Cheung paused. "Either way, I wanted to thank you for helping my grandmother after the explosion. I'm not sure she would have made it without you."

Herron nodded, and they headed inside. While he took a spot at the bar, Cheung gave a small wave to the barman and then headed out back.

The wait was a long one, and the barman ignored Herron, even when he held up a hand to order a drink. It was clear he'd only be served if the leadership said so.

Herron sighed and looked around.

The bar was packed to bursting, filled with people and drinks and laughter. The rest of the street was the same. Herron wondered idly if things would change when the mainland took over. While people had their leisure time under any regime, even one as oppressive as the PRC, he wasn't sure the relatively hedonistic pleasures of Hong Kong would survive the transition.

An hour passed, although Herron gave up on the idea of a drink long before that. The bar got busier then, later in the night, it thinned out as patrons headed home to sleep before work the next day. He was just about ready to give up on the effort entirely when the barman slammed down a bottle of local beer in front of him.

"Thanks." Herron raised the beer and took a sip, his eyes on to the barman the whole time. "Ready?"

The barman nodded and jerked his thumb in the direction of the back room. "You better not keep them waiting."

Herron almost made a crack about how long the barman had made him wait to quench his thirst, but he left it alone. Instead, he carried his beer to the back of the bar and through the curtain that separated the sections. On the other side was a small room dominated by a hardwood table.

Six people sat around it, its surface covered in maps and beer bottles and ashtrays and takeout containers. Five of them looked Chinese, including Cheung, but Herron was surprised to see a white female among them. She was about forty, wearing a pale-yellow cotton dress that looked out of place for a clandestine encounter in a smoky back room.

Herron sat in a vacant chair at the head of the table. Every eye in the room was on him, weighing him up, assessing his worth and his reliability. One person in particular – the Caucasian woman – seemed keen to size him up and her attention set off many professional alarm bells in Herron's head.

Once he was seated, he put his beer on the table and leaned forward. "Cheung tells me you have a problem with the Chinese government."

The woman laughed. "And he tells us you took the

time out of your busy criminal schedule to save his grandmother. Strange behaviour for a man who has a date with the death penalty."

"What can I say, she reminded me of my favourite aunt. Even the condemned have families, you know."

She smiled. "You don't remember me, do you?"

Herron scanned her face, desperate to make the connection, the alarm bells in his head deafening now. He didn't recognise the woman, but some deep part of his mind was trying to tell him there was a problem. When he came up blank, her smile widened, but she refused to let him off the hook by breaking the awkward silence.

Herron tried to seize back some of the initiative. "No, but that doesn't mean it was all bad, though..."

She snorted. "Director-General Charlesworth sends his regards, Mr Herron. My name is Zoe. It's good to see you again."

Suddenly, it all fell into place. The woman had been a junior intelligence officer on the operation to take down the Master when he'd tried to invoke the Lazarus Protocol and reform the Enclave. Herron vaguely remembered her in the operation's background, but clearly she'd come a long way in the few years since.

"You were in Bath." Herron waited while she nodded. "What the hell is a British intelligence asset doing here?"

"Simple. Britain can no longer enforce its will in Asia with its military, but we still have friends and interests in the region."

"Like keeping Hong Kong independent..."

"Precisely." She took a sip of her drink. "We were promised decades of independent administration as part of the handover of Hong Kong. Now the PRC has reneged."

"And you think there's something that can be done about it?" Herron gazed around the gathered leaders. "You think protest alone can overwhelm the power just over the bay?"

Zoe regarded him, a slight twinkle in her eye. "Protest, and the subtle application of power in all the right places."

"So where can I fit in?" Herron looked at her for a second, then at the other members around the table, unclear of the balance of power. "I want to hurt the PRC."

"You want to hurt Minister Han." Cheung spoke this time. "We need to make sure you don't hurt us in the process."

"Listen, I—"

Zoe cut him off. "No, you listen. We didn't leave you sitting at the bar for the fun of it. We've discussed your role and your motivation, weighing up your usefulness versus your notoriety."

"And?"

"And we've decided to give you a shot." The smile disappeared from her face for the first time. "Which, if successful, might lead to more opportunities to screw with the mainland. And Han."

"I'm listening."

"We know China is using the bombing as an excuse to send in troops tomorrow." She gazed at him. "We need to know the details."

* * *

HERRON WINCED as a gust of wind hit him and caused him to swing in mid-air. With a little work, he braced his legs against the wall of the tower he'd rappelled down and gritted his teeth as he waited for the wind to recede. It took a few seconds, but soon it calmed enough that he could continue down to the target apartment.

"Couldn't live on the ground floor, could you?" Herron muttered to himself as he continued his descent, which had started at the top of one of Hong Kong's many apartment mega towers. "Asshole."

Zoe, Cheung, and the other protest leaders had asked him to question a senior member of the Hong Kong Police Force – a Chinese stooge responsible for oppression of the protestors – about the route thousands of Chinese troops would take into Hong Kong. They needed to know if the troops would arrive by land, sea, or air, so they could swarm the area with protestors.

Scooping up the cop and getting him to a secure location to beat some answers out of him would take some magic. This Inspector Lao was well protected. He travelled in a convoy of a dozen police in several vehicles, while at his office and at his apartment, he was guarded by two officers loyal to the mainland. It was nothing a rifle couldn't handle, but Zoe, Cheung, and the others wanted the information Lao could provide.

That made a simple job infinitely harder.

Herron gripped the line with one hand and smoothly and easily lowered himself to the right level. It was slow going, and he had to be careful to not let any further gusts blow him in front of a window and expose him. Otherwise, he just had to hope the black tactical gear that he wore would shield him from any keen eyes in another tower.

Down and down and down he continued. He paused now and then to brace against more threatening gusts of wind until finally he reached the target – level twenty-two. Suspended in mid-air, he assessed the target residence and decided it was safe enough to land on the balcony.

Herron manoeuvred himself on the zipline and, using a little of his own momentum, he landed on the tiled surface as softly as a cat, barely making a sound. He tied off the zipline to the balcony rail; he'd need it again to get out of the apartment, and he wanted to know exactly where it was when the time came.

Crouched down, he drew the silenced pistol the leaders of the protest movement had provided. The lights inside the apartment were turned on, which both gave him the ability to see in and destroyed the ability of anyone inside to see out, but it was no real advantage. The television was on and there was a half-finished beer on a side table next to the sofa, but he couldn't see his target.

He stayed low, beneath the balcony side rail and behind a decorative trellis, covered both from anyone looking out of the apartment or across from another building. He waited – five minutes, ten – wanting to be sure about what he'd encounter. Ideally, that meant eyes on the target before he moved in to strike. But after twenty minutes, he still had seen no one. Patience was one thing, but he couldn't wait forever.

He had to move in.

With a sigh, he climbed to his feet and advanced to the glass door. As quietly as he could, he tested it and was pleased to find it unlocked, sliding open quietly on well-maintained runners.

The cold, conditioned air from inside the apartment hit him in the face like a slap. He stepped inside, eased the door closed behind him, and advanced down the hallway to the rest of the apartment, his pistol aimed out in front of him. Conscious that a few cops were always near his target – likely outside the front door of the apartment – he moved as quietly as he could, ready to pounce on Lao the moment he found him.

The apartment was large by Hong Kong standards. Besides the kitchen and lounge area, there looked to be two generous bedrooms and a decent-sized bathroom. Herron checked the first bedroom on his left – empty – then the second bedroom on his right. Also empty. That left only the bathroom, which sat at the end of the hallway, its door closed.

The light spilling from beneath it, and the strained grunts from the other side made Herron think he'd found his man.

He kept the pistol aimed squarely at the centre of the bathroom door, about where he'd expect the chest of the average-sized male would be when the door was opened. Finally, the toilet flushed, the tap ran, and a middle-aged man emerged from the bathroom, his eyes glued to the phone in his hand. At least until he noticed the weapon aimed at him.

"Using your phone while you're in there is disgusting." Herron's voice was quiet and cold. "Do you know how many germs the average toilet has?"

To his credit, the crooked cop was smart enough not to yell for help with a gun pointed at him. "And my apartment contains one more germ than a minute ago. Who are you?"

"There'll be plenty of time for that." Herron stepped forward and held out a hand, the pistol still aimed at Lao's chest. "Give me the phone."

Herron was pleased Lao didn't hesitate to hand the device over. He pocketed it and then gestured for the crooked cop to move into the main bedroom. Lao cop did so without complaint, which was a slight surprise given there were two armed officers somewhere nearby. Likely, he didn't want to eat a bullet while he waited for the cavalry to arrive.

The master bedroom was decked out with expensive furniture that looked far above the paygrade of a city cop, no matter how senior. It was a dead giveaway Lao was on the take, although perhaps the more obvious evidence was at Herron's feet: a line of high-quality boots that peeked out from under the bed.

Herron surveyed them, then looked at Lao. "I'm guessing each one of those pairs would cost a thousand US dollars?"

"Or so." Lao shrugged. "Let me go and I'll arrange it so that you have enough money to buy a thousand pairs. Ten thousand pairs. Whatever you want."

"I bet you would." Herron scoffed. He didn't need further evidence that Lao was corrupt, but he was happy to have it, anyway. "You know, my old man was a cop, and he never had boots that fine."

Lao's face hardened as he seemed to realise where Herron was taking this. "I—"

"I asked him about it once." Herron continued. "He said, 'Son, the only cops in Baltimore with fine shoes are the ones on the take.' It seems applicable now, too..."

Lao kept quiet. A senior cop in the HKPF, he'd come to the attention of the protest leaders years ago, but yesterday had confirmed to them his place in China's plans. He had ordered all his men out of the blast zone only an hour before the bomb went off. Not only had that denied the people caught in the explosion the help they needed, but it was a dead giveaway that Lao had known what was coming.

And that meant he had a hotline to Han in Beijing.

"So, Mr Fine Boots, let me try this on for size." Herron stepped closer and jammed the pistol against his forehead. "You've worked to undermine the HKPF from the inside, slowly turning it to Beijing's side."

Lao didn't respond.

"Along with the island's chief executive, you orchestrated the new law to give Beijing the power to seize and try any Hong Kong citizen they want. Politicians, journalists, civil rights campaigners – anyone inconvenient."

Still, Lao said nothing.

"And when the inevitable backlash and protests occurred, you provoked and inflamed the situation with rubber bullets and tear gas and a refusal to listen or take a backward step."

Again, silence.

"And then you helped pen the protestors into a tight space of a few city blocks, so when the bomb went off, the maximum number of your countrymen were killed or wounded."

No answer.

Herron pressed the barrel harder into Lao's head.

"All so that you could invite thousands of troops in from the mainland to clench their iron fist around the throat of your own home."

Expecting Lao to keep his mouth shut again, Herron remained quiet until the weight of the silence compelled the cop to speak. "I did what I had to do."

"So said any collaborator during the entire history of humanity." Herron let the words hang heavy for a moment. "You had a choice, and you sided with the devil who'd steal your freedoms."

Lao laughed. "The chief executive, her cabinet and the leader of the police force have sided with the mainland. If I refused to toe the line, I'd simply be replaced. Why not get some nice boots out of it?"

Herron shook his head in disgust. "You could have stayed out of it. You could have sided with the protestors and saved lives."

"The protestors can make as much noise as they like, but with no international support their cause will wither and die."

"They have support," Herron replied. "They have me."

"And nobody else able to do anything more than wave a placard or hurl a slogan." Lao smirked. "No western power will interfere, because nobody wants to fight a war with China."

Herron knew, deep down in the pit of his stomach, that Lao was right. It was one thing for the United States and the other western democracies to joust with China on the frontiers of its sphere of influence, in Fiji or the Pacific Ocean or elsewhere. It was quite another to meddle in matters right off the Chinese coast, despite the breach of the treaty with the United Kingdom.

Except for Herron and some covert help by British intelligence, Hong Kong was on its own.

Herron clenched his jaw. "Get off the bed and slowly walk out to the balcony."

Lao's eyes narrowed. "Why?"

Herron half squeezed on the trigger, and Lao got the hint.

They reached the balcony without fuss, the guards outside unaware and Lao doing nothing that might cause him to eat a bullet. Only when they were on the balcony, with Lao's back against the rail, did the cop finally speak.

"You're going to shoot a police officer in his own home? How do you think that will look to the public?"

"Not if you tell me when and where the Chinese troops will be arriving." Herron gripped Lao by the throat and pressed the pistol against his skull. "If you lie, you're going over the side."

"That's all you wanted to know?" Lao laughed. "Noon tomorrow via the Hong Kong–Zhuhai–Macau Bridge, right in time to celebrate the destruction of the protest movement..."

Herron opened his mouth to ask what Lao meant, but before he could speak, he heard a loud shout behind him. Keeping the pistol pressed into Lao's temple, he turned to see two uniformed HKPF officers inside the apartment and drawing their own weapons, shouting at him in Cantonese.

They had him cold.

5

————

With a split-second in which to act, Herron pistol-whipped Lao before ducking low and scrambling behind the cover of the large trellis he'd hidden behind earlier. Shots boomed in the close confines of the apartment as he moved, the windows shattering and the bullets slamming into the concrete side rail that protected those on the balcony from the long drop to the ground. He made it behind cover with no holes in him, but that didn't solve his bigger problem.

"If you want your boss alive at the end of this, you'll back the fuck off!" Herron's shout rang out over the sound of the pistols, but when the reply came back in Cantonese, he knew he was wasting his breath. "Shit!"

More shots pounded into the trellis and the sidewall. While none hit him or Lao, Herron was still in a sticky situation: trapped, with critical knowledge of an imminent attack on the protest leadership, against two shooters who'd probably called for reinforcements.

"What now, Mitch?" Herron looked around for a way to escape or turn the tables on the cops. "Think!"

He glanced around the balcony. It was sparse. There was a wooden table with two bench seats, a clothesline, and an outdoor grill with a small gas bottle attached. The limited toolbox did little to inspire Herron's creativity, but he'd made a career out of doing more with less. And, to make matters worse, Lao was slowly coming around.

Locking eyes on the gas bottle, he formed a plan. In the darkness, he shuffled low towards the barbecue and disconnected the line that connected the fuel supply. Then, popping up, he hefted the bottle into the apartment. Huddled back under cover, he heard a window shatter and the *bong-bong-bong* sound of the gas bottle bouncing across the apartment's wooden floor.

The cops didn't notice the danger they were in and kept shooting. Herron unscrewed the silencer on his pistol and fired two shots into the air. The gunfire from the apartment stopped as the two cops sought cover of their own. Quick as a flash, Herron emerged, his eyes searching for his target.

The gas bottle had come to a stop at the base of the kitchen breakfast bar – not exactly what he'd intended, but good enough. He fired two shots into it and then ducked back down as the bottle exploded in a shower of flame and shrapnel, the blast lighting up the balcony.

Herron peered into the apartment to see the cops, soot smeared and in disarray, but shielded from the worst of explosion by their own cover, retreating to the front door.

He had his chance to escape, but now the fire he'd started was imperilling him and Lao, licking out onto the balcony. They were trapped, too high for a fire truck ladder to reach and with no way for crews to get inside the apartment quickly enough to save them. While the rest of the building would be fine – evacuated by an alarm and aided by sprinklers – Lao was screwed unless Herron helped him.

He waited a few seconds to be sure the cops were occupied with their own survival, then rose from behind cover once again. The inside of the apartment was ablaze as the flames spread and filled the enclosed space with smoke. The cops were nowhere to be seen, driven off by the most basic of human fears: a primal desire to run from fire.

They probably thought they had him bottled up, so were happy to wait in the hallway for backup. Or for him to burn to a crisp. He would not wait for them to figure out what he had planned. As soon as he was sure they wouldn't fire blind through the flames and the smoke, he made his move.

He returned to where Lao lay and grabbed the abseil line tied to the balcony rail. "We're going to take a brief ride, you and I..."

He worked quickly. It took a few moments to manoeuvre the still-groggy cop into position, but his special forces experience had given him plenty of practice in securing wounded or unconscious people in abseil harnesses. A little elbow grease and a few choice swear words, and he had Lao ready to go.

With a grunt, Herron gripped Lao under his arms and lifted him off the ground. As he hefted the cop up, Herron chanced a glance back to the apartment, which was now fully ablaze. Through the flames, he could see the cops again, back and ready for a second try at him.

When they realized what he was trying to do, they opened fire.

"Fuck it." Herron lifted Lao up onto the balcony, wrapped his hand around the abseil rope and took a deep breath. "It would have been so much easier to kill you..."

As shots pounded into the concrete nearby, Herron jumped.

He fell, Lao going with him, held safely in place by the harness. Herron had to rely on his grip strength and a little luck. They dropped a few floors quickly, then the rope's safety catch kicked in.

With a sharp lurch, Herron found himself hanging in the middle of the Hong Kong skyline with the barely conscious second-in-command of the city's police force. He gripped the rope tighter, then chanced a look up. The glow of the fire spewed out from the apartment he'd helped set ablaze.

A look down confirmed residents of the tower were already evacuating...

... and that it was a long way to the ground.

Herron reached up to manipulate the controls that would slowly ease them to the ground. "Here goes nothing."

And at that precise moment something – the fire or a bullet or just some malicious bastard back in the apartment – cut the rope above him.

They fell – fast – and with no way to stop it. Lao's screams left no doubt he'd finally woken up.

While Lao had no chance, Herron had a split-second to save himself. He lifted his hands above his head and flailed for something to grab on to. His fingers snagged a balcony side rail.

"Shit!" Herron yelled as his grip held, the sudden deceleration almost tearing his arm from its socket.

Lao's howls grew more faint with each passing second, then abruptly ended, replaced by the wail of a car alarm, piercing the night, and revealing exactly where the cop had landed.

Herron stared down long enough to confirm there was no movement from Lao, then turned his attention to the balcony he was currently suspended from. His eyes widened when he saw an entire family – two adults and three children – staring at him from inside the apartment, frozen in shock. He smiled in what he hoped was a friendly manner, then pulled himself onto their balcony.

He had to get the hell out of this building. Clearly, only a few levels had been evacuated so far – or else this family had ignored the alarm. He walked over to the glass that separated him from the family and tried the door.

It was locked.

"Oh, come on." Herron looked at the father of the family, then pointed at the door, then mimicked a prayer gesture. "Let me in, buddy."

The father hesitated, but eventually he nodded and unlocked the door. He slid it open a little on its rail and stuck his head out. "Why are you here?"

"There's a fire upstairs. Haven't you heard?"

"You go from balcony-to-balcony warning people about a fire?" The man frowned at Herron. "I'm not letting you in…"

Herron drew his gun, just enough for the man to see it.

It was a pretty good sales pitch. The man took a step back and admitted Herron through the glass door.

"Thank you." Herron stepped into the apartment. Then, with another quick smile at the children, he made straight for the front door.

* * *

BY THE TIME Herron reached the ground level, one member of a long conga line of people forced to snake down the fire stairs, the whole tower was in the middle of a total evacuation. Several fire trucks had parked out front and cordoned off the area, their strobing red light bars giving the lobby the feel of a nightclub.

He kept his head down and his hands in the pockets, doing his best to avoid attention from the residents who were headed out of danger and the firefighters headed toward it. By now, law enforcement would have found the body of their inspector, and the two cops he'd kept at bay with the explosion would have reported that they'd seen him. The last thing he wanted was to be spotted so close to escaping.

He had to stay free at least until he'd warned Zoe, Cheung, and the other protest leaders that the hammer was about to drop.

Out on the street, the by-now familiar Hong Kong humidity hit him in the face. There was no opportunity to pause outside, and the stream of people carried him along whether or not he liked it, right past the car Lao had landed on. A dozen cops were huddled around it, their faces stern, but no attempt was being made to resuscitate their leader.

There was no point.

Herron cursed quietly. Lao's death had removed any chance of extracting more information about the arrival of the Chinese troops or the attack on the protest leadership. He'd simply have to run with what he had, but without a phone number to contact Zoe or Cheung – or a phone – the best he could do was to hurry to the bar to warn them.

The further he got from the apartment tower, the easier the journey, the street becoming less of a crush and more the standard Hong Kong crowd. Nobody was going as far as Herron, keen to stay near their homes while he was keen to get away, and as he stepped on the giant public escalator that would take him back towards Lan Kwai Fong, he relaxed.

He held the side rail, took in the sights and wondered how they'd change once the mainland's control was absolute and the current freedoms enjoyed by the locals were finally crushed. It showed the fickle nature of freedom, which some enjoyed because of a vote or a revolution, but others were denied because of a war or an international compromise.

The thoughts kept Herron occupied until he stepped off the escalator at the point nearest to Lan Kwai Fong, where he was scheduled to meet the protest organisers, hopefully in time to move them before the attack. Although they'd be shocked by Lao's death, the information he'd procured would keep them safe for at least a little longer.

Herron walked down the street with his hands in his pockets. On his left and on his right, the dive bars that the area was famous for dominated the streetscape, although there was less going on than the last time he was here. It was a Sunday night, so the bars were only sparsely occupied, but it was also likely the protests and the bomb had kept people away.

Most importantly, there was no sign of any imminent attack on the bar that housed the protest organisers.

He was almost at the bar when he felt it, a sensation few humans on earth ever experienced. A combination of God-given talent and decades of experience, it made Herron's spine tingle, his arm hair stand on end and his trigger finger itch. It was impossible to ignore, and anyone in his business who did so earned an early ticket to a shallow grave.

Taken with Lao's warning, it made him alert as hell.

He used every reflective surface around him to scan his environment and try to spot the threat. A store window, a parked car's side mirror, a seated woman's small makeup mirror. Each provided a chance to look at the world behind him. But there was no obvious threat – neither someone a little too close nor anyone with a visible weapon. Whoever had triggered his senses had at least an ounce of skill.

Someone was on his tail, but he couldn't find them.

He needed to get to the bar fast, to warn them about the imminent attack, but he was no use to anybody if he was assailed before he got there. And he couldn't pass on the information by calling or messaging; the protest leaders eschewed electronic communications. His only option was to evade the tail then go to the bar.

He just hoped he could shake the trouble and make it back to warn them before the hammer dropped.

About to pass a metro station, he suddenly cut a sharp left and entered it. He walked through the small collection of convenience and drugstores on the level above the rail platform, then stopped to purchase a ticket to ride the subway. Within a minute, he was through the ticket barrier and on his way down the escalator to the platform.

Yet his sense of danger didn't relent.

Whoever was onto him was still there. They hadn't hesitated to follow him down onto the subway, an enclosed environment with fewer escape points than the streets outside, which meant they were sticky pursuers who'd stay on him no matter where he went. That gave him two choices to free himself and make his way back to the rendezvous.

Fight or flight.

He leaned heavily on the right handrail of the escalator. The black rubber was cool to the touch, a contrast to the rest of his body, which felt like a furnace after his acrobatics at the apartment tower and the laps he'd been doing in the humidity of Lan Kwai Fong. Some of his sweat remained on the handrail, an unwelcome surprise for the next traveller to come along.

At least the conditioned air was a comfort down here, but as with all breaks in his walk of life, the relief was temporary.

He reached the end of the escalator and stepped onto the platform, his moment of relaxation over. Immediately, he disappeared amidst the press of fellow commuters, who were too polite to stare at the sweaty westerner among them. Trains arrived on either side of the platform, passengers came and went, but Herron stayed anchored to the spot.

He was right where he wanted to be.

* * *

HERRON CLOSED his eyes to let his senses uncoil for a second; they'd worked overtime to identify the threat. After five seconds, he took a deep breath, then exhaled heavily.

"Showtime."

He opened his eyes, turned on the spot and quickly scanned around him, filtering out the commuters who waited for trains or had their heads buried in their cell phones. Only then did senses honed to a razor's edge by decades of the hardest training and experience possible find them – two of the Chinese operatives he'd left behind at the bomb site.

They'd changed their clothes, now dressed as Hong Kong Police Force officers, with matching powder-blue shirts and black dress pants. It was a smart disguise, letting them go anywhere and do whatever was necessary to catch Herron. It also allowed them to grip the Glock-17s at their sides as they inched ever closer to their target.

Herron waved, showed them he was on to them...

... then he turned and pushed his way through the crowd. With each step, he half-expected to hear the boom of the operatives' pistols and feel the pain of hot lead entering his back. But his bet on their reluctance to shoot a man in the back in public proved to be correct. No shots came, and he was able to use the cover of the crowd to distance himself from his pursuers.

The same senses that had zeroed in on the first pair of operatives sensed another pair now, closing from a different direction. Both pairs shouted at the crowd in Cantonese and at him in English. They thought they had him in a trap, a vice-like grip that would squeeze him into submission.

But that's where they were wrong.

Herron pulled his pistol from his pocket, aimed at the ceiling, and fired. His shots blasted the overhead tiles to dust and sent the civilians on the subway platform into a blind panic. They screamed and ran in a million different directions, past the overwhelmed operatives, to clamber up escalators to the street above. Most importantly, they blocked sightlines and put further stress on the operatives' decision making.

As the chaos unfolded around him, Herron took a few strides to his left and stepped onto a train that was about to depart. The operatives shouted after him, and one even fired into the chassis of the train, but the panic he'd caused on the platform had bought Herron the time he needed to get away. All the noise was silenced when, a second later, the doors closed behind him and the train pulled out.

Where he was going didn't matter. All that did was that the operatives hadn't followed.

He took the time between stations to take a breather and cool down a little, crushed among the terrified passengers who had heard the shots but not seen it was he who had fired them. Then, as the train slowed for the next station, Herron moved to the doors.

The train stopped, the doors opened, and Herron left the carriage surrounded by panicked passengers. As they scrambled for the escalators and safety, he went with them, hidden in plain sight as, a moment later, the next train pulled in. There would be operatives aboard, but they'd be struggling to stay on his tail, given he had a one-train lead on them.

Three would likely stay on and get off, one at a time, at the next three stations.

One would get off here.

It was the best possible way for them to make use of their numerical advantage, giving them four chances to pick the tail back up, versus the single chance if they stayed together as a pack. But for Herron, it increased his odds of evading them for long enough to make it back to the bar in Lan Kwai Fong. One pursuer was much easier to deal with.

As he neared the top of the escalator, his theory was proven right: the next train arrived and one of the four PRC operatives stepped off, eyes sweeping the platform.

Confident that he'd evaded the bulk of his minders, Herron emerged in Causeway Bay and started on his way back to the bar. There was still one operative to deal with, but Herron had a plan for that, walking in a slow and obvious straight line towards the place he hoped to shed this last barnacle.

He crossed the street and walked a short way to the entry of Din Tai Fung, the place he'd eaten right before visiting the bomb crater with his minders. The restaurant was on the second level and taking the escalator up, he felt the tingling sensation that told him the operative was behind him.

But not for long.

Inside the foyer, he asked for a table by the rear window, then followed the server to it. Only when he was near it did he freeze on the spot and look behind him. There, nearer to the door, the operative-dressed-as-a-cop had just entered, his gun drawn, and his attention fixed on Herron.

"You're cornered!" The operative shouted in broken

English. "If you give yourself up now, we can find an opportunity for you to redeem yourself!"

By killing thousands of innocents? No way.

Herron sprinted towards the operative, who raised his pistol and shouted again for him to stop. If his words had been bullets, Herron would have been filled with holes... but Herron had correctly assessed his foe's enthusiasm to create a scene was low.

At least part of the reason was the camera crew Herron had noticed the day before, set up to film a show about the head chef. They were still there, their eyes and their cameras alike tracking the scene in front of them.

Even though Herron was a wanted man, the operative wouldn't kill someone in front of a rolling camera and risk angering Minister Han. The politician only wanted Herron on camera when it suited him. After all, China had planned their move against Hong Kong for decades; the last thing Han would want was his men to shoot up the most prominent restaurant on the island.

The camera crew provided Herron with a force field of sorts, the chance to attack then melt away without retaliation.

Racing past tables filled with other diners – who looked curious and scared in equal numbers – Herron closed to strike. Even then, his foe hesitated, his body locked up between following his ironclad orders and its natural biological defence mechanisms. Herron didn't wait for him to decide; he gripped the operative's wrist and twisted it until the pistol fell. The agent cried out, the pain finally spurring him to fight back, but Herron delivered a brutal headbutt that ended the matter quickly.

And, just like that, he was free of his tail again.

He reached down to take the faux cop's pistol, turned, and sprinted to the window nearest to the main road. As he got closer, he slowed just enough to grab a chair and heave it toward the glass, which shattered into a million pieces, littering the sidewalk below with shards.

Cops – real ones now – were arriving in the restaurant behind him, called at the behest of the restaurant staff. They shouted at him to halt, some even firing their pistols as Herron charged for the window. He burst through the window, hurtling into the brightly lit street that only a day ago had been the site of a huge protest and bombing. As he flailed through the air, he desperately looked for something to break his fall.

This time, he was out of luck.

He slammed into the side of a bus that had slowed out front of the restaurant, the blow rocking him, but not as bad as a bullet would have had he stayed inside the restaurant. He collapsed to the ground, a small crowd of locals milling about to check he was okay. From the restaurant above, cops shouted down at the street and tried to find a clear sight line for another shot.

Herron shook off the effects of the hard landing, keeping low to put the civilians between himself and the cops. He knew the HKPF officers wouldn't shoot into a crowd of innocents, no matter how much they'd been corrupted by the mainland, so with the concerned locals still asking after him in Cantonese, he slid underneath the bus and emerged on the other side.

Now shielded from the gunfire, but certain help would be on the way, he sprinted off into the night. Only when he was a few blocks away did he stop to check that he hadn't taken a bullet, pleased to find the cuts and grazes from his landing were as bad as the damage got. It hadn't been his most subtle escape, but it had done the job.

If he hadn't proven himself to the protest leaders by now, he wondered what it would take...

6

It took Herron about a little time to get from Din Tai Fung to the rendezvous, by which time the area had further cleared out, only the alcoholics and the die-hards left on the prowl. That suited Herron fine; he wanted to be sure nobody else picked up the tail, and less foot traffic made it harder for a pursuer to hide in plain sight.

Yet while his senses didn't warn of anyone on his tail, he still felt on edge.

He stood on the corner opposite the bar for a few minutes and watched. A handful of patrons came and went, yet he saw nothing that justified his dread. After a while, it was decision time. But given he wanted to keep alive his chance for revenge against Han and the Chinese Government, and that if he turned around and left he would have no resources to call upon, it was a straightforward choice.

He'd face any threat head on, like he always had.

He crossed the street and entered the bar. Once again, he sat on a stool at the main bar, yet this time he had the attention of the bartender and a beer in front of him almost instantly. The bartender smiled at him and jerked a thumb toward the back room, signalling to Herron that he was welcome in the inner sanctum.

He pushed his way through the curtain and saw the same faces as before staring at him. "Don't you bastards ever sleep?"

"Rarely." Cheung's voice was deadpan. "And not at all for the last few days, given all that's at stake with the mainland pressing so hard."

"The army is moving in tomorrow morning via the Hong Kong–Zhuhai–Macau Bridge." Herron sat heavily in a chair. "And Lao hinted to me that an attack on this group is imminent."

The group shared a look of trepidation, all except Zoe, the British intelligence agent. Like Herron, she had made a career out of this business. None of the others were professionals: for them, thousands of troops from the mainland and a targeted strike against their leadership raised the stakes of the game considerably.

"Well, we'll deal with that like we do every other problem." Zoe grinned, trying to bring some positivity back to the group. "You caused quite a scene..."

Herron shrugged. "Lao would still be alive if his guards hadn't popped off. Anyway, I got what you wanted. I'm just annoyed I couldn't get specifics about the attack on you all."

"We knew it would come, eventually." Zoe had a twinkle in her eye as she replied. "Now we need to decide how to proceed, given our timetable has been advanced much faster than expected."

The locals looked at each other; it was Cheung who finally broke the silence. "We have to halt the protests.

Otherwise, our followers will be dead meat. Probably us, too."

"Then Han wins," Herron said. "You need to lean into the PRC's plan, rather than back down. Put a hundred thousand people on that bridge and dare them to drive through you."

"Easy enough to say," one of the others chimed in. "But when flesh and bone is standing in front of metal and guns, I know what my money would be on..."

Herron sat back, his contribution made. He was in this for the fight and would take it to Han and the mainland, whether or not the protestors joined him. If they didn't point him at a target, he'd find one himself. But they each needed to decide if they were ready to push all their chips into the middle of the table; the consequences for them and their cause if things really went to hell would be catastrophic.

The conversation swirled around for almost an hour. Zoe, like Herron, mostly kept her mouth shut. Her role was to support the locals to fight for their freedom, but if the locals decided to lay down their arms and go home, she had no purpose in Hong Kong anymore.

She didn't have a personal vendetta to settle like Herron did.

They discussed options, and in the end, sanity prevailed. There was a consensus around the table to meet the arrival of troops with the largest and most concentrated protest yet. A last attempt to overwhelm the resolve of the mainland and garner the support of the rest of the outside world through a display of sheer numbers and determination.

That, plus a refusal to hide themselves away in the face of the coming attack.

That was the part of the plan Herron had a problem with. Common sense, his training and his experience dictated the leadership should go to ground, but all of them refused to hide away from danger while they asked their followers to front up to Chinese troops. They committed to dispersal, so at least they couldn't be rounded up in one place. After this meeting, there'd be no more contact for some days.

It was a plan full of risk, but their only other choice was abject surrender. They spoke deep into the night about every element of the plan, hammering out the kinks until they were exhausted. When they were done, everyone knew their role, including Herron.

Yet the whole time he sat there – and even made a few observations – he couldn't escape the unease in the pit of his stomach that he'd felt on the street corner outside. For a man who'd made a life's work out of death and destruction, the looming sense of doom unnerved him. But without a specific threat to focus on, all he could do was invest in the plan he'd agreed to play a part in.

With the meeting concluded, Herron stood with the others, determined to catch some sleep prior to the fireworks in the morning. He let the others clear out until only Zoe was in the back room with him. When he gestured for her to go before him, she shook her head and stood in his way, blocking the narrow space to the exit, arms crossed over her chest.

She tilted her head sideways. "Where are you staying tonight?"

"I'll find somewhere."

"My hotel room has sofa..."

Herron nodded. It was as good an option as he was

going to get, and she seemed happy to offer it. Without further delay, she turned and headed out into the bar proper. Now alone in the back room, the uneasy sensation in Herron's gut returned. Pushing it to one side, he followed her, the last to leave the back room.

And the last to have a pistol aimed at him.

Herron froze, instantly assessing the situation. The four operatives who had dogged him across Hong Kong had the entire group of conspirators surrounded. One was covering the barman and the other patrons in the bar, but the bulk of the guns were pointed right at Herron and his compatriots, ready to decapitate the protest movement in a few quick seconds, if they wanted to.

Their leader, Wei, stepped forward. "It's over. All of you get on the ground."

"I'm the one you want..." Herron held his hands up. "These people are innocent. Let them go."

"Innocent?" Wei snorted. "This is the protest leadership. We were going to send police to do the job later tonight, but you led us right here. We thought we would save some time."

Herron's heart sank; he'd sped up the destruction of the group. He looked around for an edge, but there was none to be found. He could reach for his pistol and maybe take out one of them, but all that would achieve was his own death and plenty of collateral damage. So, as the protestors complied with the order to drop to the floor, he prepared to join them until he noticed Zoe staring at him.

She mouthed something to him: "Wait for it..."

Herron frowned, then his eyes shot to the barman. He didn't look like a threat, but he was only being overseen by one of the four operatives, and his eyes kept drifting to Herron and the others. It gave the man a chance, albeit small, to cause a distraction and spring them loose.

But he did more than that.

As Herron eased himself to the floor, the barman moved fast. In a flash, he seized a nearby bottle of wine, smashed it and jammed the broken neck of the bottle into the nearest operative. The agent tried to raise his weapon, but the bottle had bit deep, and he was already pumping out blood from his wound.

With one operative out of the fight – at least for the moment – Herron ducked low and dragged Zoe to the ground. Shots popped and filled the bar, the barman and several of the protest leaders falling as bullets took them. It wasn't a battle: the locals were unarmed and easy targets. Caught without cover, they were cut down in seconds, their conspiracy destroyed in an instant.

Herron moved fast enough to upturn a table and avoid being hit immediately. With Zoe next to him, he'd survived the first exchange, but the operatives were ascendant. He drew his pistol, rose from behind cover and popped off at the agents. Zoe, producing her own weapon, did the same. Their shots hit one operative in the chest, dropped him, and forced the others to retreat behind cover.

Knowing this was his one chance to get out of the situation, Herron grabbed Zoe by her shirt and pulled her to her feet. Together they ran toward the large bay window that fronted the bar onto the street outside; Herron raised his pistol and fired several times, which shattered the glass.

Shots cracked behind them as they jumped through

the window and ran down the street. The few civilians who'd been in the area this late at night squealed and fled for cover, their panic cluttering the street and masking Herron and Zoe's escape.

To Herron's surprise, the operatives made no move to pursue. Perhaps they were content with a solid night's work, annihilating the leadership of the protest movement.

When he felt they were at a safe distance, Herron slowed to a stop and turned to Zoe. "I didn't mean to lead them here..."

"Even if you did, it doesn't matter now. We're alive and the others are dead." She paused, panting. "Anyway, it's not the first time I've had a mission wipe and it won't be the last."

"What now?"

"Back to my hotel to change and wash the blood off me. You coming?"

* * *

WHILE HERRON WAS EXCITED they'd made it out of the bar, he knew they might not make it much further.

Each step put more distance between themselves and the operatives, but the streets were filled with police cars and cops, as well as army trucks and soldiers. Troops moved in squads up and down each major street, and occasionally sallied into an office or apartment tower and emerged with a citizen in cuffs, no doubt a protestor or a sympathiser on a list of people the mainland wanted quietened. Every time a truck or a squad car was full, they'd blaze off down the street, headed for who knew where.

Herron watched them as they sped past, the cops and the troops stoic and proud, the citizens desperate and scared. Suddenly, it was apparent that the special status Hong Kong and its citizens had enjoyed inside the Chinese political system for a few decades after British control had come to a rapid and terrible end.

He figured those who'd been arrested would end up in some prison or another, maybe even the one he'd been held at; the result would be the same. Without the protest leaders to organise, their voices would be silenced, their cause would die, and their home would become a jewel in the crown of the Chinese Communist Party, its proud history of freedoms and peaceful co-existence a sad historical footnote.

"They're making a statement," he said to Zoe.

She nodded. "We knew they were bringing in troops tomorrow and you figured out where, but now they've stepped up their timetable. There's going to be twenty thousand troops on the street by midnight..."

"Heads up." He turned from her to look straight ahead. In his peripheral vision, he continued to track the soldier who'd taken a keen interest in them. "Soldier eyeballing us at three o'clock."

Zoe tensed a little. "How do you want to handle it? I'm out of ammo, and my spares are back at the hotel room."

"Not sure guns blazing is the best approach here, anyway. It's me they want, so I'll peel off and try to lead him away while you go on to the hotel."

"Okay..." Her voice trailed off, like she wanted to argue but knew the plan was sound. "If you lose him, meet me in Room 1407 of the Crowne Plaza."

Herron nodded and immediately turned down a

side street, hopeful that if he disappeared from the view of the soldier, his place in the man's mind would also wane.

Hopeful but not confident.

As he walked, he used every reflective surface around him to take in the surrounding scene. For a second or two, it looked like he might have evaded the soldier, but then the uniformed man landed on Herron's tail.

"Shit. Turn back, you bastard."

The soldier continued after him.

Herron wasn't sure he'd been made: more likely, the soldier had just spotted a pair of Westerners together amidst the crackdown and taken an interest. It was an assumption he ran with for now, because if the soldier really had identified him, it meant there were a hundred more on the way, and he'd have bigger problems within moments.

Herron turned down an alleyway and swiftly hid behind a dumpster, ready to ambush the soldier and try to take him down. There was no alternative against a man armed with an assault rifle in the middle of a city street. The alley gave him a few advantages – it was pitch black, and he was well concealed – plus he most likely had better close combat skills than a Chinese infantryman. But the trooper had the rifle, and plenty of friends nearby.

The soldier appeared at the end of the alleyway and headed into it, each step as loud as a cannon shot to Herron's sharp senses. Herron waited, poised to strike, but when the soldier was a few steps from his position, the man's radio crackled in Mandarin.

The soldier stopped, peered around, then spoke into

the radio. It was clear from the tone of both sides of the conversation that the soldier was the junior rank...

... and he was getting his ass chewed out for wandering off.

Herron smiled as the soldier retreated, but he didn't emerge from cover for a full fifteen minutes. When he did, he spent another hour walking random patterns of the streets, to make doubly sure he hadn't attracted more attention. When he was satisfied, he headed for the hotel and made it up to Zoe's room. He knocked, and as she let him in, he realized she was on a call.

"I can wait outside..." He mouthed the words, but she shook her head and held the phone out to him. He looked at her quizzically, took the phone and put it to his ear. "Hello?"

"I thought I told you to stay off the grid." The familiar voice of Director-General Charlesworth filled Herron's ear. "Fucking fine job of it you've been doing of that for the last few months..."

Herron smirked. Although they were nominally enemies, he'd gained a lot of respect for Charlesworth in the time they'd spent together hunting the Master and destroying the Enclave. "Well, I lost my boat..."

"So I heard." There was a pause. "Anyway, lad, I appreciate your effort to get Zoe out of that sticky situation. Having a British agent captured would have been most unpleasant."

"My pleasure." Herron looked at Zoe and raised an eyebrow, as if to ask what the point of the call was. She shrugged. "I thought you were more focused on internal security, Director-General."

"I got a new job overseeing MI6, and I moved some of my best people from Five over with me to Six."

"What can I do for you, Director?"

"Just wanted to hear your voice for myself, son." Charlesworth paused. "I sincerely hope you're still able to talk this time tomorrow."

When Charlesworth killed the call a moment later, Herron tossed the phone back to Zoe. "No problem making your way back here?"

"No. I was just bringing the Director up to speed. I assume you had no trouble with that soldier on your tail."

Herron shook his head. Seemingly satisfied with his answer, she turned and headed for the bedroom; a few seconds later, he heard the shower start. Running his hand through his hair, he headed for the sofa, which was in the corner of the room near the balcony.

He sat down, the weight of the world on his shoulders. It felt like a lifetime since he'd woken up in the hotel room the previous day. He closed his eyes.

The next thing he realised, Zoe was standing in front of him with a towel wrapped around her.

"You really know how to make a woman feel wanted..." She raised an eyebrow. "I thought we'd do a few things before we slept..."

Herron looked at her, puzzled, having to work hard to avoid his eyes drifting down her body. "You said your hotel room had a sofa..."

"I didn't say you had to sleep on it. But if you really feel strongly about the matter, then I won't stop you..."

Herron thought about it for less than a second and then climbed to his feet.

* * *

HE WOKE to the sound of gunshots outside, the *chatter-pause-chatter-pause* bursts of assault rifles. In an instant, he was out of bed, pistol drawn. A glance back to the bed showed Zoe doing the same, their night of bliss now far in the rear-vision mirror as they were forced to focus on the new day.

And the war zone outside.

Herron moved to the suite's living room, past the sofa where he'd intended to sleep, and opened the door out onto the balcony. Pistol gripped by his side, he looked out on a city ablaze. Smoke rose into the sky from three dozen fires – lit by protestors or sparked by the conflict – while the rattle of gunfire continued to carry on the wind.

He moved to the edge of the balcony and looked straight down. The street, in the heart of Causeway Bay, was filled with protestors armed with placards standing up to a line of Hong Kong police who'd stopped them from spilling into the main shopping precinct. The only difference to previous days was the dozen bodies that littered the no-man's-land between the two forces.

"They've stopped playing nice." Zoe stepped up behind him a few minutes later. She held a cup of coffee for herself and another for him. "Thought you might need it."

"Thanks." Herron took the cup, lifted it to his mouth and took a hefty chug of the coffee. "What now?"

"Well, last night was a onetime performance, I'm afraid. It's against organisational policy for an intelligence agent to sleep with the most wanted man in the world twice."

"At least we made it count." He turned his attention

back to the struggle on the street. "Do the protestors have any hope without their leaders calling the shots?"

"None. And I just got an alert from Charlesworth. The extra Chinese troops have flooded into the city this morning. They're rounding up protestors, moving into key positions, crushing all dissent."

Herron groaned. Leaderless and directionless, the protestors who were brave enough to continue to take to the streets were easy prey for the mainland forces.

"What now?" Herron repeated, in the hope she might have a more professional answer. "I wanted to help you take a shot at Han and the others, but I don't know where to aim."

"I don't know, Mitch." She sidled up alongside him to look out over the destruction. "Do you ever wonder how many moments in history were decided by the actions of covert operatives?"

"Not really." He paused, but she did not fill the silence. "I've been involved in a bunch of them, so plenty I guess..."

"Well, this one hurts." She took a sip of her coffee. "This mission is wiped, and I've been ordered to bug out."

Herron turned to her, surprised she would give up on the mission so easily, given it involved the breach of a treaty signed with her country. "Stay."

"Why?"

"We can throw some spanners in some works. We probably can't stop China getting what it wants, but we can make it a hell of a lot harder."

She shook her head. "It's over, Mitch. We gave it our best shot. I'm on a flight this afternoon to London. You should get out while you still can."

"I've got no resources and nowhere to go." He cast his eyes down on the carnage below as the cops gunned down more protestors attempting to break their lines. "And I've got a score to settle."

"With Han?" She scoffed. "He's coming here to take control of the island's government. No more self-rule. No more transparent courts based on the rule of law. No more freedoms. No more life."

"Not just Han. His goons as well." Herron gripped his pistol a little tighter. "When and where can I get to him?"

"He's untouchable." She drained her cup. "Anyway, I need to go. You've got a formal offer from the Director-General to join me if you want to enjoy the protection of Great Britain."

"He wants me to travel with you to Britain and then work for him?"

"You're not just a pretty face." She reached out to touch his cheek. "Charlesworth is offering the same terms as before – if you work for Britain, you'll be protected by Britain."

Herron stepped back from her. Suddenly, it was clear why Charlesworth had wanted to talk to him the previous evening. It had been a proof of life call, just like in Bath, when he'd ended the Master and destroyed the Enclave. Charlesworth was trying to control him, and if he agreed, he'd be deployed around the world to take down the enemies of Britain.

A pawn in someone else's game again, a puppet dancing to another's tune.

He'd done it before. He'd killed and almost been killed hundreds of times. On the command of others, he'd pulled triggers, detonated bombs, stuffed people into trunks and completed many other nasty tasks. Some victims had deserved it, probably, and some of those moments of history Zoe had spoken about had probably swung in a better direction because of his actions.

But others had surely swung the wrong way, and it was no longer the life for him.

Any actions he took now were his own.

"My days of killing for others are over." Herron's voice was firm. Final. "If you ever get sick of it, look me up."

She was visibly taken aback. "I'm nothing like you, Mitch. I fight for the security of my government and the safety of my people."

"I thought that once as well." He finished his coffee, put the cup on the balcony railing. "There's four Chinese operatives on my tail who think the same."

She sneered. "Low blow."

"Just don't let all this consume you."

"You're too cynical for your own good." She gave a thin smile, clearly forgiving his cheap shot. "I know why I fight, and this is my job, not my life."

"Lucky." Herron let the word hang for a moment, heavy and solemn. He'd never had that choice. "Just let me have a shower and I'll get out of your hair."

Herron headed back inside the hotel room, showered and, with no clean options available, dressed in the same clothes he'd worn the day before. Leaving the bathroom, he found Zoe seated on the bed, her bags ready to go at her feet.

He grinned. "Not the first time I've had a woman pack up while I shower."

She rolled her eyes. "And this isn't the first time I've helped a dead-beat boyfriend..."

She threw a small bag at him, and he caught it reflexively. "What's this?"

"A little farewell gift to help you achieve your goals." She got to her feet. "If you somehow survive, meet me at the airport tonight and I'll get you out on the 9.00pm flight to London."

Herron nodded, grateful for the offer, although he had no intention of taking her up on it. "You did good work here. Don't take the loss of Cheung and the others to heart. It wasn't your fault."

"Thanks, but that won't do anything to bring them back." She picked up her bags. "Or hurt the bastards responsible."

"You leave that to me."

7

Herron kept his hands in his pockets as he approached Hong Kong's Legislative Council Complex. When he was near enough to see the impressive facility, which looked like a black spaceship, he stopped and leaned against the wall of an abandoned store. All around him, the protests swelled, the streets filled with an angry mob that was being met with violence and gunfire.

The mood differed from the previous times Herron had been amongst the protestors. There was less singing and fewer patriotic signs, more shouts, and makeshift weapons. Since the bomb had gone off and their leaders had been slaughtered, the mood amongst these people was a powder keg of anger, and he was sure Han wanted them to explode.

It was Herron's job to prevent that.

The Legislative Council complex was where the ceremony would be held to celebrate the formal handover of authority to the mainland, and it was harder to get inside than Fort Knox. A first ring of security was provided by the Hong Kong police, who'd erected roadblocks and personnel barriers to keep the protestors at bay. Behind that ring of steel, uniformed PLA troops stood watch.

It was an impressive display of might, with guns by the hundred and armoured vehicles by the dozen; even Herron would normally struggle to breach them. Thankfully, although the cops had rendered the home of Hong Kong's democratically elected government inaccessible to the protestors and anyone overly hostile, Herron had more tools than violence at his disposal.

He pushed himself off the wall and casually walked on down the street. The crowd of protestors increased the closer he got to the building and reached critical mass a block away from it. There, hundreds of people were pressed up against a barrier manned by the cops, and Herron had to push his way through, all elbows, until he reached the front.

"Stay back!" A cop shouted at him. "If you try to force your way past the barrier, we're allowed to use deadly force."

"Not trying to get shot, pal, just doing my job." Herron huffed and puffed, doing his best to seem put upon by the surrounding protestors, rather than someone who shared their cause. "I'm a reporter."

"Press?" The cop stiffened. His eyes darted around, looking for anything that might reflect badly upon him or the PRC. "No camera?"

Herron rolled his eyes. "Not all journalists work for television, buddy. You know one of the main reasons for the decline in political cov—"

The cop held up a hand. "You should have used the journalist gate, like your colleagues..."

"Look, all I want is to write a nice little fluff piece on the event today and you're busting my—"

"Do you have a pass or not?"

Herron reached into his pocket, never taking his eyes off the cop, then flashed his pass. The officer inspected it and took a step back, allowing Herron past the first ring of defence. He stepped through the gap in the barrier, sure he had the attention of every protestor and cop in the vicinity, then pocketed the pass and continued deeper into the compound.

He had the same experience at the next two checkpoints, making it past the soldiers and then the civilian staff that controlled access to the building itself. It showed him the respect officials in authoritarian states had for credentials. Nobody questioned him. Better for them to shrug their shoulders, go with the flow, and, if questioned by those in power, swear the guy had shown the right ID.

He'd got the press pass from Zoe. It had been in the bag she'd tossed him, along with a few wads of local currency and a note: *Thought you might be able to use this. Meet me at the airport if you change your mind. Otherwise, make it count.* He'd smiled when he'd read the note, which made him think of their night together, then had pocketed the gear and settled on his plan of attack.

It wasn't a complicated one.

Within fifteen minutes, after more queues and security checks, Herron found himself in the lobby of the Legislative Council building, with an entirely different crowd of people. These were the hand-selected and the rent-seekers, those who'd welcome or benefit from increased PRC control over the island, as far opposed to the views of the protestors outside as it was possible to get.

In just a few brief minutes, the event would begin: the signing of the final handover of full authority to the mainland. The dignitaries were mostly already seated, and those who still mingled in the lobby were being ushered to their seats with announcements in Mandarin, Cantonese, and English. Everyone complied with the instruction, including Herron.

Seated at the back of the cavernous hall, he watched as Han and Au Jin Ren – the chief executive of Hong Kong – spoke about their desire to bring the island and the mainland together; about their hope that the new laws would ensure everyone lived under the same rules that had proven so prosperous for the rest of the PRC; and about their belief in the peace the extra troops would help secure.

Polite applause followed each speaker, a pointed contrast to the violence on the street. As he looked around, Herron could see dozens of sycophants in business suits and cocktail dresses, all happy to see their freedoms signed away to enjoy the benefits of patronage. An end to the protections Britain had negotiated for the locals years earlier. The betrayal of millions of people distilled to a single pen stroke by the island's chief executive.

It was a triumph for Chinese foreign policy and Han knew it, if judged by the wide smile on his face as the document was signed. He'd overseen a foreign policy agenda that had swept across Southeast Asia and the Pacific, bent other states to his will through military or economic or political coercion – or sometimes a mix of both – and now secured the return of the greatest treasure of all.

And Herron could do nothing to stop it.

But while nothing and nobody could keep the PRC from exercising its own unique brand of dominance over South-East Asia and the Pacific, Herron could destroy its architect. Han had propped up the General in Fiji and the hijackers in the Philippines. He'd locked up political prisoners, even killed them – and Cara Sargent – to spite Herron. He'd ordered his men to plant a bomb in Hong Kong and then detonated it.

And those were just the crimes Herron knew about.

Han had proven to be ruthless, and the human gene pool would be better without him in it. But to kill the man would make him a martyr and result in further predations on Hong Kong and its people. Instead, Herron would take from Han the thing he probably valued more than his life.

His reputation.

Herron reached into his pocket. There were a hundred other journalists gathered in the surrounding seats, focused on their devices or their notepads, none of them paying him any attention. That changed when he tapped the man next to him on the arm and handed him a small piece of paper.

The journalist frowned and looked down at the folded sheet. "What's this?"

"You're Ken Dinnane?" Herron waited while the journalist studied his face, recognition finally dawning. "Right?"

"You're Herron. The terrorist."

"Molly sends her regards."

"Molly?" Dinnane's eyes widened and took on a

haunted look. He knew his instructions to the young journalist to pursue Herron's story at any cost had likely ended her up in prison. Or worse. "Do you know where she is? Do you know if she's alive?"

"She's dead." Herron let the words hang heavy. "And you owe it to her and to the world to get her story out, no matter the cost."

A range of emotions played out over Dinnane's face. Grief. Anger. Guilt. "What am I going to find?"

"The story of your life. Proof that the Chinese foreign minister has been complicit in the death of thousands of political prisoners. Get the story out or I'll find you."

"What?" Dinnane looked up at him, but Herron was already making his way to the end of the row. "Wait, you're—"

Herron didn't look back. He'd done all he could. The piece of paper contained a URL for a server that contained drone footage of executions at the prison, hundreds of them, along with information that identified each victim. It was the last part of the gift from Zoe: a dossier collected over months of British surveillance of the prison where Herron had been detained. Proof Charlesworth had been watching him closely.

Given Molly was one of those executed on the footage, Herron was certain Dinnane would get the story out. And when it was made public, the dossier would make Han – and most of the rest of the Chinese leadership – a pariah outside of China. He'd be the subject of Western financial and travel sanctions, leaving him poorer and crippling his ability to travel outside of his homeland. For a man with his position –

foreign minister of a great power – that would be a blow impossible to recover from. It wouldn't be long before the regime sought his replacement.

Herron was handing Dinnane the scoop of a lifetime.

He was giving the United States a home run.

He was giving Molly and the other prisoners a small amount of justice.

And he was giving Han a giant middle finger.

He could have used the dossier to negotiate his own freedom and safe passage from China, but as he stared at the stage, he was glad he hadn't done that. After a moment, the Chinese foreign minister spotted him, the only person standing in a room full of seated officials. There was a frozen moment, an entire conversation played out silently, in seconds...

Then Herron walked away.

He had no problem exiting the room or the building. The PLA and the Hong Kong Police Force were focused on keeping the protestors out of the event, not preventing those already inside from leaving. Within a few minutes, he was out in the fresh air and through the security cordon, back amongst those he'd tried so hard to help.

As he walked further from the Legislative Council Complex and toward Causeway Bay, he felt uneasy. In Fiji, he'd caused carnage, but it had been justified to remove the tyrannical control of the General and stave off the encroachment of the PRC. That place was now free, under democratic rule, its people happier and with a better future. In the Philippines, he'd dealt a fatal blow to the hijackers before he'd been captured.

But here had been different.

Here, he'd tried to help another island stave off the control of the PRC, but this time, he'd failed. Despite his efforts, thousands of troops had arrived from the mainland, the leaders of the local protest movement had been slaughtered, and a document had just been signed to rubber stamp PRC authority onto the territory and end the modicum of freedom they'd allowed its people for a few decades.

His decapitation of Han's career would do nothing to change that.

He admired the fight in the protestors. Although they had only a small amount of support from British Intelligence, they'd shown impressive mettle. But it had all been for nothing. They were dead or in prison and their cause was lost. Herron was once again adrift without home or purpose, a modern ronin wandering the land for his next fight.

He was done with being retired. But he was also done with causes.

* * *

HERRON PRESSED his back against the wall and kept his hands in his pockets – one wrapped around the grip of the pistol – as he watched the television in the corner of the bar. On it, the broadcast of some local soccer game had been interrupted with a newsflash showing the handshake between Han and Chief Executive Au Jin Ren that had sealed the fate of the island and its residents.

While the patrons jeered and shook their heads at the news, Herron couldn't understand a word of the excited chatter that filled the bar. None of them looked his way, the sole westerner in the bar, too consumed in their own futures to realise the most wanted man in the Earth was amongst them. The man who'd fought hard to help them stay free and failed.

But also the man who'd set up a fireworks show of his own to mark the handover.

The news feed shifted to a video already familiar to Herron. It showed grainy, black-and-white camera footage of what looked to be a prison shot from the air. As the picture zoomed in, it was easy to see a few dozen people huddled together in a hole... and then those same people drop to the ground as the prison guards who encircled them opened fire. The video cut back to anchors, who sat in stunned silence.

It was the same story in the bar, where patrons stared at the screen and each other.

Herron figured the same film was playing on every television in Hong Kong and much of the rest of the world, as the video proof of China slaughtering political prisoners was disseminated. He was glad Ken Dinnane had been as good as his word and used the significant reach of his network to get the images out into the world.

Herron had done what he could, and now it was time to go.

He drained his Coke and headed for the exit, pausing out in front of the bar to look left and right.

Headed in his direction were the three remaining Chinese operatives.

For a second after he saw them, no one moved.

Then he ran, bolting down the alleyway next to the bar and into the shadows.

This close to the docks, the entire area was filled

with warehouses, separated by blind corners and dark alleyways. It was like a maze, the only place in Hong Kong without a crush of people, and the perfect terrain for Herron to finish up his last piece of business.

The whole time he'd walked from the Legislative Council Complex down to the docks, he'd been sure to look up at every security camera he saw. Based on Lao's statement, the entire island had a network of cameras running facial recognition software, and Herron had let himself be tracked to exactly where he wanted the operatives to find him.

The stop at the bar had simply been a refreshment break. To let them catch up.

He snaked his way through the alleyways, only seconds ahead of Wei and the other operatives. He didn't know his way, but nor did his pursuers. And here he was, free of the security cameras and able to take advantage of all his other natural advantages over the kill team.

In the forest in the Philippines, Herron had been at an enormous disadvantage against four agents. He'd been armed with only a pistol and his wits, whereas his foes had operated under the protective curtain of sniper cover, while the ground team packed long guns, night-vision goggles and other tactical gear. He'd taken down two of their number before Wei had shot him in the gut – a decent but disappointing effort.

This time, things would be different.

Herron had retrieved his pistol from where he'd left it after he'd departed the Legislative Council Complex. He was down to his last dozen rounds, but here, in the shadows, he had advantages far more dangerous than a pistol. He had training and experience and a God-given talent he'd bet against the Chinese operatives any day of the week.

Unlike their encounter in the forest, the men were armed only with pistols and had no tactical gear.

He'd have their number.

He turned to look over his shoulder and saw the trio round a corner as he did the same. They were close – close enough – and now he had to hit the next note of his composition. He ducked out of sight and bolted to the end of the alleyway, where it split in two directions. Taking a second, he chose his direction and kept running.

Shots fired, pounding into the bricks beside him, but in the dark of the alley, none found flesh. Herron jagged in another direction, glad he hadn't yet eaten lead and glad his suspicion was confirmed – now Han had completed the handover, the previous restriction on lethal force had ended.

Over and over, he snaked through the labyrinth, allowing the operatives to stay close enough that they'd be confident they had him in the bag. The first key part of his plan had been to get them into unfamiliar territory. The second was to keep them confident enough not to call reinforcements.

The last part was to split them up. And his plan was a simple one: not the result of great tactical planning or superior technology, but an example of the most basic fieldwork.

He reached yet another intersection, turned down it, and stopped.

This time, instead of a quick sprint to the next junction, he took shelter in the door nook of a warehouse. It was bathed in darkness, almost pitch black – he'd be hard to spot if anyone came past.

He kept to the darkness as the three operatives reached the intersection and paused for just a second; they hadn't seen which way he'd gone. Predictably, they chatted for a moment in Mandarin and then split up. Wei went left – away from Herron – while the other pair went right, heading towards him.

Both agents had their pistols raised as they stalked ahead, more cautious now they had lost track of him. They moved in unison – well trained – and whispered to each other in Mandarin.

The whole time, Herron held his breath and kept deathly still; he wanted to keep his position concealed until the very last moment.

They passed him, and he emerged from the shadows silently. His footfalls as quiet as a whisper, he wrapped his arm around the neck of the man on the left. As he pulled tight, he raised the pistol and aimed at the other operative, who had turned and was raising his weapon. A quick tap of the trigger halted that threat, while a second tap and a shot to the head made sure of it.

That left him alone with the man he was choking out.

Herron jammed his pistol into the operative's back, a slight amount of pressure on the trigger. Simultaneously, he choked the agent harder, as the man thrashed and tried to free himself. A boot slammed down on Herron's left foot and the operative's ass bucked back into him, the classic one-two move people trained in self-defence used to free themselves.

The third move, Herron already had covered.

"If you try to headbutt me, I'll snap your neck." Herron whispered into his ear. The agent hesitated; as Herron had suspected, it wasn't just Wei who spoke English after all. "I want you to call Wei and tell him I'm here. Understand?"

"I understand," the man croaked. "I'll tell him now."

The operative spoke quietly into his wireless headset. Herron was sure it was a call for Wei to help him and detail of the situation. He didn't much care about the specifics; all that mattered was drawing the last remaining enemy to him.

The second the call was done, Herron snapped the operative's neck.

As the dead man dropped to the ground, Herron returned to the shadows. He waited, again in silence, as Wei arrived and cautiously advanced down the alleyway. Every few steps, the lead agent paused, his senses no doubt on edge, before moving on.

Until he found the bodies on the ground and froze.

Herron advanced out of the shadows and pressed his pistol against Wei's skull. "You've reached the end of the line, my friend."

Wei tensed a little and dropped his pistol to the ground. "Put that gun down and we'll finish this man to man."

"You didn't give me that opportunity back in the Philippines or in Lan Kwai Fong. Why should I offer it now?"

As Wei opened his mouth to respond, Herron pulled the trigger.

* * *

HERRON USED the bolt cutters he'd purchased from a hardware store to cut a hole in the chain-link fence. It was topped with razor-wire, and he was sure there were surveillance cameras that would spot him either now or later, but he only needed to avoid the attention of port security for a few minutes.

As he'd walked to the rendezvous after he'd taken out Wei, he'd briefly thought about taking Zoe up on her offer. He could get a cab to the airport, meet her in the lounge and make his way to London with far less risk than the path he'd ultimately chosen. But he'd stuck with his original decision; going with Zoe would end with him in service to the British.

With him killing for another master.

Instead, he'd chosen a path potentially far more turbulent, one that would begin with a clandestine meeting in the shadows of one of the world's great commercial ports. There, he hoped to book a ticket to anywhere but here. It offered fewer guarantees than a business class flight to London, but he'd take the chance that one of the few people he'd ever been able to trust would remain reliable.

He climbed through the hole in the fence, tossed the bolt cutters on the ground, and moved through the shadows. A few times, he had to skirt wide around stevedores working the busy port, but a slow and cautious approach got him to where he needed to be – on the far side of a warehouse at the back of the port, looking out over the water.

"You better damn well show up..." Herron whispered under his breath. "Or this is going to get a hell of a lot hairier..."

Right on time, the sound of a small boat signalled

that his stay on the island was almost at its end. Herron stayed in the darkness as the boat bumped up to the dock, and someone stepped off it. The figure whistled three times – the signal Herron had said to use – then waited. Herron gave it a few seconds to be sure it wasn't a trap.

"I got your message." The man's voice was neutral, neither positive nor negative, his words a simple statement of fact. "I thought you understood the Philippines was a onetime deal?"

"Things changed." Herron emerged from the shadows, revealing himself to the newcomer. "A lot changed."

"Now you want another 'Get Out of Consequences Free' card?" Captain Jerome Laidlaw asked. "It's not so simple, Mitch."

"Sure it is. Give me a ride on your boat. Drop me off wherever the hell you like on the way back to Yokosuka. Forget about me."

That had been the plan, when Herron had used Cheung's e-reader to email Laidlaw from a newly created account. He'd revealed details about a previous mission they'd conducted together – things only Laidlaw knew – to prove his identity, and asked Laidlaw to sail to Hong Kong under cover of darkness to get him out.

He had set the rendezvous for a few hours after the handover event was supposed to occur. He'd figured by then he'd be done working for Han or done trying to stop him, and it would be time to get the hell out of Dodge. He didn't care where he went – it didn't matter – but he needed to get away from this island and from China. But his friend had to put the last piece in place.

"I'd love to," Laidlaw said, "but one of my crew blabbed the last time I helped you out and I had all sorts of people who work for all sorts of U.S. agencies pissed off at me for letting you slip the noose. When you showed up in Beijing, in the hands of the Chinese Government, it made those same people even angrier still. It put me into a bit of a corner, Mitch."

Herron frowned. Suddenly, a business class flight to London with Zoe didn't seem to be the worst idea. If Laidlaw's feet had been put to the flames the first time he'd helped Herron, there was no logical reason for him to be here.

Moving slowly, so he wouldn't be noticed in the near-darkness, Herron reached behind his back and gripped the pistol in the waistband of his pants. "Why are you here then?"

"Because those same agencies told me to be," Laidlaw replied. "You need to come with me, Mitch."

Herron drew his pistol, quick as a flash, and levelled it at Laidlaw. "I'm walking away."

"No, you're not."

Suddenly, Herron was blinded by floodlights from behind Laidlaw. A dozen voices shouted at him to drop the pistol or they'd shoot.

He kept the pistol aimed at his friend, even though he couldn't see well enough to pull the trigger. He was surrounded and exposed, out of the shadows and in the light, with nowhere to run and no way to hide.

"I trusted you, Jerome!" Herron hissed, hurt by the betrayal of one of the few people he'd ever trusted. "What now?"

"Well, that's up to you." Laidlaw's voice was cold and

clinical. "Resist and get shot or put down the gun and come with me."

"Come with you to be killed or pressed into service?" Herron paused, and the silence all but confirmed it. "I told you I was done."

"Done?" Laidlaw laughed. "After my crew member blabbed, I almost lost my career. Then you pop up in public, get caught, and contact me to help you out. They gave me less of a choice in this than you have."

Herron lowered the pistol. He couldn't fire.

Laidlaw walked up to him, took the gun, and clamped a hand down on his shoulder. "Good call. Now let's get out of here. You've got work to do."

ABOUT THE AUTHOR

Steve P. Vincent is the USA Today Bestselling Author of the Jack Emery and Mitch Herron conspiracy thrillers.

Steve has a degree in political science, a thesis on global terrorism, a decade as a policy advisor and training from the FBI and Australian Army in his conspiracy kit bag.

When he's not writing, Steve enjoys whisky, sports and travel.

You can contact Steve at all the usual places:

stevepvincent.com
steve@stevepvincent.com

ACKNOWLEDGMENTS

Not a long list of people this time around. I spent the entire time it took to draft this book in some sort of COVID lockdown, so I should actually thank Mitch Herron - you kept me sane, buddy.

As always, thanks to Gerard and Dave for the beta read, Pete for the edits and Stuart for the cover.

And to you, the reader - it's a pleasure, as always.